A Rain of Fire

Enders hurled himself up and out of the trench, running pell mell out into the heart of it, Thompson machine gun blazing.

"Enders!" Hjelmstad shouted. "No. Get the hell back!"

But Enders hadn't heard that—really hadn't, his bad ear—and kept charging into the flying bullets.

And down in the trench, Hjelmstad yelled, "Well, cover the fool, goddamnit!"

Yahzee, watching his bodyguard running fearlessly—recklessly?—into the teeth of enemy fire raised his carbine and began squeezing off rounds. Beside him, the Texan, Chick, was letting go with the BAR; the whole Second Squad did their best to lay down some cover for this kamikaze run. . . .

Enders dove and rolled and came up almost on top of the spider hole at left, and when the Jap within looked up, lifting the lid, Tommy gun fire filled the sniper with lead and his hiding place with blood.

WINDTALKERS

A Novelization by MAX ALLAN COLLINS
Based on a Screenplay Written by JOHN RICE & JOE BATTEER

HarperEntertainment
An Imprint of HarperCollinsPublishers

This is a work of fiction. Names, characters, places, and incidents are products of the author's imagination or are used fictitiously and are not to be construed as real. Any resemblance to actual events, locales, organizations, or persons, living or dead, is entirely coincidental.

HARPERENTERTAINMENT
An Imprint of HarperCollins*Publishers*
10 East 53rd Street
New York, New York 10022-5299

Copyright © 2001 by MGM Studios. All Rights Reserved.
All photography copyright © 2001 MGM.

No part of this book may be used or reproduced in any manner whatsoever without written permission except in the case of brief quotations embodied in critical articles and reviews. For information address HarperEntertainment, an Imprint of HarperCollins Publishers Inc.

ISBN: 0-06-000096-1

HarperCollins®, ■®, and HarperEntertainment™ are trademarks of HarperCollins Publishers Inc.

First HarperEntertainment paperback printing: October 2001

Printed in the United States of America

Visit HarperEntertainment on the World Wide Web at
www.harpercollins.com

10 9 8 7 6 5 4 3 2

For Tom Weisser—
who has introduced so many
to the wonders of John Woo

———————————————

And when he gets to Heaven
To St. Peter he will tell
One more Marine reporting, sir
I've served my time in hell.

Epitaph in a cemetery at Lunga Point

In the house made of dawn,
In the house made of evening twilight . . .
With your moccasins of dark cloud, come to us.

Prayer to the god of thunder
(translated by Washington Matthew), *Navaho Legends*

1

GUADALCANAL WAS NO PAGE OUT OF A TRAVEL BROCHURE. True, with its blue-green spine of mountains, the luxuriant darker green of its jungle, and the faded greens and browns of grassy plains and ridges and coconut groves, the Island—as the U.S. Marines in the summer and fall of 1943 came to call it—could fairly be described as a tropical paradise.

But to the Marines, Guadalcanal was just an ugly goddamn perimeter about five miles long and three miles wide. The Solomon islands, lying a few degrees south of the equator, provided their American guests a wet hot climate; frequent rains and unremitting heat turned this paradise into a steamy, pestilence-ridden hell, decorated with *kunai* grass as tall as a Marine and as sharp as a

K-bar, a jarhead's fighting knife . . . the two main uses of which were vicious infighting and opening food tins.

Guadalcanal was a real tourist trap, all right— foul, fetid swamps, humid jungles alive with insects as big as lizards and snakes, and lizards and snakes bigger than that. Crocodiles awaited at the mouths of rivers, and malaria-infected mosquitoes attacked the invaders, whether American or Japanese, without prejudice. Few of the Marines on the Island avoided malaria, not to mention other tropical diseases, and almost every fighting man fought fungus infections as well as Japs.

The men who battled . . . and survived . . . on Guadalcanal—and the number of those clashes can only be estimated—would carry these injuries and tropical diseases into further fighting and, the lucky ones, into post-war civilian life. They would fight their battles again and again in sickness-tinged fever dreams.

Some of them still do.

On the morning of September 8, 1943, the First Raider Battalion under Colonel "Red" Mike Edson went ashore at Tasimboka. The enemy— convinced a major landing was under way—fled the scene, leaving supplies behind that the Americans, who could damn well use them, confiscated. Soon the Marines re-embarked, sailing to Lunga Point, their pockets stuffed with tins of Jap meat and bottles of sake; upon arrival, the Marines learned that the enemy was on its way to them, hacking through the jungle, with reclaiming their captured airfield in mind.

Marine manpower was too limited to maintain a continuous perimeter on the Island, and all the troops could do was guard the more obvious approaches to the airfield (renamed Henderson Field in honor of a Marine pilot killed at Midway). Corporal Joseph F. Enders was part of a group of reinforcements brought in that night along the beaches of Lunga Point, on September 12, when a horde of Japanese attacked.

His lieutenant had been killed in combat the night before. None of the sergeants made it off the landing craft, leaving Enders in charge of his first command—a godforsaken beachhead on the ass end of nowhere, draped in a thickness of fog, as if all the smoke of the war's battles had been wrapped up in one big ball and dropped on that sorry stretch of sand.

A dark, lanky loner, with a sharp-featured face and sorrowful eyes, Enders—like many of the men under him—had a touch of malaria that hellish night. He would survive the bloody battle in a dense fog penetrable only by bullets; but the memories would be similarly draped in fog, and would return to him again and again in the months ahead, to where he could no longer distinguish between them—dream and memory, memory and dream. . . .

The fog floated, so thick you could almost grab onto it; the world was a blur of gray, with only the sounds emanating from deep within its mysterious non-landscape achieving any clarity—and then merely dull, hollow sounds: boondockers slogging across sand, the clank of gear, the sucking in of breath.

Only the occasional gunfire attained sharpness in this smeary world—like the tracer rounds, burning incandescently through the enveloping gray, like tiny ghastly Fourth of July rockets. Enders perceived them as if in slow motion, one to his right, then another to his left, no time, no need, to duck . . . no name on these bullets—not his name, anyway, not yet. . . .

His men were behind him—that much he knew . . . and little else . . . as he raised his Thompson submachine gun and blasted into the fog, fanningly returning fire in the direction of those tracer rounds, hoping to God (or the devil if need be) that the unseen enemy might catch that burning lead, not some poor leatherneck bastard who'd wandered off course in the haze.

Enders seemed to be firing forever, the weapon's recoil slowed, bullets inching from a white-hot barrel. Was he in a dream? Or just in that nightmare of combat that threatens, at any instant, not to wake you screaming, but rather put you to permanent sleep?

A shriek pierced the fog, as sharp—sharper—than the sound of bullets, some of which had found purchase in the chest of a Japanese soldier who'd materialized out of the fog, so as not to die unnoticed, it would seem.

The shot soldier's scream banished that sloweddown sense of the corporal's, sharpening Enders's perception, as more Japs materialized, phantoms appearing out of the fog, in their uniforms the color of brown wrapping paper, their kepis with sunshielding swatches waving at their necks like white flags, only these bastards were hardly surrendering. They were shouting, *"Banzai!"* and "Die, Marine!" as the glint, the icy wink, of flashing bayonet blades danced like lightning in the gliding vapor.

His Thompson chopped several of them to kindling, but one demon, coming at his blind side, lunged forward, Enders catching the bayonet glint too late to react in time . . .

. . . but the blade was not fated for him. The Jap had instead jabbed the spike of steel into Private Tommy Kittring's shoulder, as he stepped up alongside the corporal. Kittring (of Atlanta, Georgia) frowned, as if he'd been stung by one of those damn malaria skeeters, and his gaunt, boyish face . . . so near Enders . . . did not register pain, not immediately.

Then Kittring screamed, and fell to his knees, as

Enders fired over him, the deafening Thompson chatter turning Kittring's assailant into a spray of red mist against the gray.

Another scream ripped through the fog's fabric, but not the man Enders had turned to meat. Private Hasby, Al Hasby from Milwaukee, was clutching his elbow, over a shattered forearm, scarlet ribboning down over his wrist. The kid—and he was just a kid, so many of them were, seventeen, eighteen— looked at Enders the way a child who's hurt himself turns to a parent for an explanation. Why had God set things up like this? Why pain? Why such horror?

Private Mertens—Bill Mertens, Denver—was blasting with his M-1 toward the phantoms . . . the Japs had faded back (momentarily?) . . . and now his trigger clicked on an empty chamber. The stocky jarhead, his eyes wild, yelled to the man in charge.

"Runnin' out of ammo, Joe! Gotta pull back!"

Enders, hoping none of these little yellow fuckers lurking in the fog spoke English, sprayed the gray curtain with another lethal Tommy burst; he seemed not to hear Mertens, over the machine-gun's roar . . . but in reality, he was ignoring the son of a bitch. They had their orders, didn't they? Hold the beach.

Nothing ambiguous about that.

Young Kittring's voice was shrill, almost girlish: "Jesus, Corporal! He's right! Look around, man!"

Reloading, Enders took this advice, looking around, and despite the hanging fog, he could make out the overwhelming, demoralizing sight of what had become of his unit: half a dozen exhausted men, scared shitless, standing in the midst of their dead and dying buddies, a dead Jap flung here and there as well, the sand damp with scattered pools of blood. The streaks of smokelike fog made it less real, but no less horrible.

Mertens was at his sleeve. "Shitcan this, Joe— gotta get the fuck out. Nobody else needs to die here."

Enders gave Mertens a hard look, glanced at the others, his handful of remaining men; their eyes were heavy on him, dragging him down. He did his best not to show it, to keep his face a carved stone mask.

On his knees in the sand, like he was praying for a miracle, Hasby was clutching his bloody elbow with a hand turned entirely red, now—he had tears on his dirt-smudged cheeks, and he was pleading: "Joe . . . I wanta go home. . . ."

Feeling his jaw muscles tense, Enders swung around and blasted the fog again, the thunder of the Thompson making the demoralized men around him flinch. Who the fuck didn't want to go home? Goddamn babies . . . babies . . . just babies. . . .

"We got orders," he said, wishing to hell he

weren't the one in charge, wishing this fucking decision were someone else's. "Hold the beachhead, they said—and that's what we're going to do."

Enders strode over to Hasby and the kid's eyes widened ever further, holding up his blood-soaked good hand, as if afraid Enders was going to slap him; instead, the corporal slapped his own .45 automatic into that red hand.

"On your feet, Marine—you got a job to do." Swinging around toward the other men, Tommy gun in hand, he yelled, "We all do!"

Mertens and Kittring jumped back, afraid maybe he was going to unleash the Thompson's power on them.

"Hold the goddamn beach!" Enders yelled, veins pulsing in his forehead, cords standing out in his neck.

And as if the enemy (not his own men) had heeded his advice, Enders turned to see a horde of the brown-suited specters emerging from the fog, with rifles and pistols and machetes at the ready as they charged, the latter the blades they'd no doubt used to carve through the jungle to this beachhead. Bayonets and rifle butts flashed in the eerie non-light as Corporal Enders and his men battled the brown-uniformed ghosts; their ammo soon gone, their K-bars in hand, the Marines slashed at the foe, and when knives got knocked from their grasps, the Marines slugged it out, fist against pistol and blade.

Somewhere in the shroud of fog, Mertens yelled, "Goddamn you, Enders!"

These were Mertens's last words, a machine gun ripping into his guts, dropping him to the sand to die with his entrails in his hands, the toy-like chatter of the puny Jap machine guns adding insult to injury.

His shot-up arm dangling, dripping, young Hasby blasted Enders's .45 wildly into the oncoming brown-uniformed tide, soon emptying the clip; the boy threw the pistol at one of his attackers, even as another was bringing a machete down, to cut through one more American weed.

Enders saw this, had no time for any pang of regret or remorse, but luckily had just enough ammo left to share a last Tommy burst with the boy's killer.

Who . . . a killer who was just a kid himself . . . fell back into the fog, as if swallowed by it, while Hasby—cut in two, literally, the sections of him flopping, plopping onto the dead fallen Mertens—formed with his compatriot a grotesque memorial of war. Not the kind of statue anyone would ever erect, however accurate and apt. . . .

Drunk with the violence and the surrealism of the fog-draped beachfront battlefield, Enders almost missed seeing the grenade bounce in alongside Kittring like a missed catch. Enders lunged across the blood-soaked sand and grabbed the grenade and hurled the thing, hoping to save Kittring and maybe even himself . . .

. . . But it wasn't much of a toss, he'd never had much of an arm for sandlot ball, and the grenade took its damn time, seemed to hang in the air as if stuck there, and when the explosion came, what saved Enders was having Kittring between him and the white blinding flash filled with hurtling shrapnel.

Corporal Joe Enders didn't even hear the explosion; rather he was just swallowed by it, and then like a seed spit out with careless contempt, into a shell hole, a crater filled with seawater, into which he splashed, and settled on his belly, seeping blood in strange, billowing patterns whose abstract beauty might have struck Enders as an ironic aspect of war, had he not been as devoid of consciousness as those around him who, unlike himself, were dead.

And when the wind came, to blow away the fog, to reveal the intertwined corpses of green uniforms and brown, of men white and yellow, Enders could not yet see the carnage-flung terrain he'd fought to hold. He lay motionless, his body a twisted sprawl, though his head, his face, lay perched on the edge of the crater, his nose and mouth out of the water, keeping him alive.

His eyes were open, but he saw nothing, at least not at first. Then, barely stirring, hardly alive, blood oozing from his left ear, he stared across the beach, watching the breeze like a gentle broom sweep the gray veil away to reveal the bodies, so many bodies, too many bodies, of his men, and of the enemy, American Marines and Japanese Imperials, some in death grips that were oddly like embraces.

His last thought, before unconsciousness took him back again, was a detached observation: it seemed in death, on the battlefield, corpses had no country.

All of this Joe Enders experienced—more than once, more times than he could count—in fever dreams as he lay in the big tent of horror that was the field hospital, into which so many, too many, casualties were crammed. Marine corpsmen did their best to staunch the bleeding, to console the wounded. Brave men wept, moaned, screamed. No one thought less of them.

Enders was just another mangled Marine, clinging to life as if to driftwood in an ocean of sharks, a heavily damaged piece of military merchandise with more bandages showing than flesh, the biggest concentration of gauze mounded around the left side of his cranium.

He felt no pain, not at the moment; and he was just woozy enough to figure out that they hadn't stinted on the morphine. A sandy-haired thirtyish doctor with a faint kind smile and gentle blue eyes took care changing Enders's dressings, and the corporal could see—behind the compassion of those eyes—the man's distress. Enders wanted to reach out and touch the doctor's arm and say, "It's okay, doc—I can't feel a thing."

But Enders could not find the energy to do that; he wasn't even sure he could talk, and anyway he couldn't summon the will to try.

Then a colonel—looking strangely out of place in this house of pain, martial crispness surrounded by so much untidy anguish—was at the doctor's side. The slender, businesslike officer waited patiently for the doctor to finish—the colonel's face not betraying any reaction to what Enders knew must be his deep, horrible wounds—and then nodded to the medic, who gave Enders a small reassuring smile, before stepping away.

Leaning over him, the colonel—he had a pale, hawkish face—said somberly, "From what I hear, you went above and beyond the call of duty, Corporal."

Enders just stared at the guy. Above and beyond?

The colonel withdrew something from his jacket pocket; he held his palm up and open, so Enders could see: a Purple Heart. Then the officer took the corporal's right hand and placed the little medal there. Enders managed to close his fist over it.

A ruptured duck, Enders thought. Hell, you could get that for catching syphillis.

As if reading the Marine's mind, the colonel said, "That's just a down payment, son. I'm putting you in for a Silver Star. . . . You earned that, and more, by my way of thinking."

"I'm . . . I'm the only one who made it," Enders said, his voice small and scratchy, like an old phonograph record. He was a little surprised to find out he could indeed talk. These were his first words since entering the Field Hospital, though he'd been conscious for some time.

The colonel nodded.

Enders stared up at the colonel, who seemed slightly uncomfortable.

Finally the officer cleared his throat and said, "God bless you, son," nodded, and walked off, cutting quickly down an aisle with misery on either side.

And Corporal Joe Enders, the cold medal tight in his fist, lay staring at the canvas ceiling, wondering if that was how you got the Silver Star in this man's war: by getting all of your men killed, and saving your own ass.

2

THE PEOPLE LIVED IN A WINDSWEPT, SACRED LAND. CRE-
ated specifically by the Holy Ones for the Navajos
(as the People were called by others), the Land of
White Brightness was part of what the white men
called Arizona and New Mexico (and took up little
bits of Utah and Colorado). To the People—in their
tongue, they were the Dineeh—this country was
less part of southwestern America than of the Fifth
World of White Radiance, marked by four sacred
mountains at its corners—reminders that men
and animals had been required to pass through
four other worlds, prior to this one . . . and that
the People were bidden to live in harmony with
the earth and its streams and plants and animals.

In 1943—only seventy-five years after the genocidal treachery of white American "hero" Kit Carson had reduced their numbers to fewer than eight thousand—the Dineeh represented the largest Indian tribe in America, with twenty-five thousand on the reservations in Arizona alone. But relative to the vastness of the land, their numbers were meager, their lives, their accomplishments, dwarfed by the awesome surroundings of twisted rock formations, exotic mesas, scorched desert, and massive mountains.

Navajo country in Arizona was one such vista of stark, rugged beauty after another, with elevations ranging between 5500 and 9000 feet above sea level, and a broad plateau given shape by buttes, mesas, gorges, volcanic necks, and washes. On the sculptured canyon shelves loomed the remnants of cliff dwellings a thousand years old; wind-stirred sand blanketed the region in irregular layers; and its yucca, sagebrush, greasewood, and grasses were interspersed with forests of pine and patches of pinon and juniper, a landscape the People shared with prairie dogs, coyotes, rabbits, rats, snakes and lizards, as well the occasional porcupine, wolf, fox and bear.

A battered bus dating back perhaps a decade, painted a neutral if vaguely military tan, rumbled down the graded shale of Klethla Valley Road, bound for the trading post at Kayenta. Hot, crowded, its passengers sat as silent as cigarstore Indians; but they were the genuine article—

Dineeh men in colorful if faded flannel shirts and blue denim trousers and dirty boots, their skin tanned bronze, some almost black, their hair long, either brightly banded or tucked under Stetsons with feathers in the hatbands, their belts studded with silver conchos. Sitting by the window, next to a seat he was saving, one of these men—Charlie Whitehorse—let his hair flow free; the biggest man on the bus, he sat back, with his arms folded and the eyes in his round face closed.

The sights along the roadway were commonplace to Charlie and the other men—though some were watching out the windows, through the red-tinged dust the bus churned up, pressing images into their memories—pictures of home for men who, despite their impassive demeanors, were apprehensive about the strange territories that lay ahead.

They were leaving behind them such familiar sights as Dineeh men riding along the roadside on scrubby ponies; of squaws weaving colorful blankets beside igloo-shaped hogans; of boys (not quite men) guarding sheep and goats. The bus was rolling through Monument Valley—a long-isolated area, a secret the People had kept, till the Hollywood director John Ford let the cat out of the bag with that movie *Stagecoach*—a valley extending north to the San Juan River and west to the Sega Mesas, arrayed with red sandstone outcroppings. Many of these stood several hundred feet high, shaped by the wind and the gods into spires and pillars and statues, rose-colored, blue-shadowed works of natural art looming over the sands like Greek ruins.

Charlie Whitehorse did not need to open his eyes to see these "monuments"—they were long since impressed in his memory, his being; he would carry this big country and its big sky with him wherever the white man sent him.

Whitehorse lived the traditional Dineeh life—he and his latest wife (he was on his third) lived in various hogans and brush shelters, depending on the time of year; he kept sheep and they would move their herds as the needs of grazing and watering made necessary. And, of course, if somebody died in a hogan, it had to be immediately abandoned or burned, since corpses—even those of loved ones—spread evil upon those who came near. Also, Whitehorse—as his name implied—was a horseman of some renown; horse racing was a popular Dineeh sport.

The man he was saving a seat for, Ben Yahzee, did not live the traditional life; a modern Navajo, Yahzee worked in one of the two new ordnance plants built near the reservation, attended night classes at the community college, and had pursued ways his old friend Whitehorse did not envy. In Whitehorse's thinking, Ben tried to be an Indian and a white man at the same time—a practice doomed to failure. Such a man was never accepted by the whites, Whitehorse felt, and began to lose touch with the People's ways, was in danger even of forgetting his own language.

Like Ben, Whitehorse was volunteering; but Charlie knew that every able-bodied Indian was being drafted, anyway, and had chosen this path because Ben had convinced him the Marines would be a better home than the Army. Also, if the country in which he lived was at war, Whitehorse—like almost every Navajo male—needed only to be shown where the enemy was. He would fight.

His eyes still closed, a tiny, barely perceptible smile etched itself on Whitehorse's lips. He knew Ben Yahzee would be waiting at the trading post with that pretty wife and their cute little boy. As much as Whitehorse admired the little family— loved them—this to him represented the depths to which his friend had sunk.

Ben had actually married the woman in the white man's church (there were thirty such churches on the reservation now!). Navajo custom allowed frequent marriage and divorce without any legal registration. Just as Dine—the language of the People—had never been written down, so were marriages written on the wind.

Now Ben was married in writing, the white man's way, with all the legal tangles that entailed. To Whitehorse, this was lunacy beyond any Peyoteinduced madness. Ben even committed that most unpardonable of cultural sins—he communicated with his own mother-in-law!

As Whitehorse reflected upon these matters, his friend Ben Yahzee—a few miles away at the ramshackle, mission-style trading post at Kayenta—used a gentle forefinger to wipe a tear from his wife's cheek.

"I will write," he said.

"I will write every day," she said.

Yahzee—a slender, slim-waisted yet strapping man in his early twenties, berry-brown, with the angular features of his warrior ancestors and the same boyish dark eyes as his young son—brushed away another of his wife's tears; but she was looking past him, now.

"Here it comes," she said, their three-year-old, little George, bouncing in her arms, laughing, pointing.

Yahzee, who wore his best flannel shirt and new denims, glanced behind him. The cloud of red-hued dust down the highway grew ever closer, marking the moments he had left with his family.

Standing behind the little family—at a respectful distance—were a dozen or more members of Yahzee's greater family, the men and women, the young and the old, of the Bitter Water People, born for the Towering House Clan. Their attire—fit for marketing their wares at the trading post or appearing at tribal headquarters, the equivalent of the white man's Sunday go-to-meeting attire— reflected the import of the occasion: the men in clean pointed boots, blue jeans, and ten-gallon hats with the ever-present feather in the hatbands, signifying the wearer's pride in being an Indian; the women in knee-high calfskin moccasins, calico skirts, loose-flowing velvet blouses, with bright kerchiefs over their braided hair.

Yahzee's wife wore no kerchief, her lovely dark hair knotted at the back of her head, her exquisite heart-shaped face free of any make-up, her beauty as natural as the country around them. Her bearing seemed calm enough, but in her eyes, panic danced—she was studying him, as if trying to memorize his features.

The bus rumbled and screeched and coughed to its stop, the men within peering out the windows on a sight they had seen again and again on this long day: a man bidding farewell to his family. Charlie Whitehorse did not look—his eyes remained shut as Yahzee hugged his wife, and then his son.

The vehicle door folded wheezingly open and, carpetbag in hand, Yahzee headed up the few steps; but before he got swallowed inside, to become just another bronze face on the crowded, broiling bus, he stopped short, and ran back to hug them again.

Wife crying. Son laughing.

Not even the driver called for him to hurry—no catcalls from the bus, either, that was not the way of these men. Their eyes turned away, giving the family a last moment alone.

Then Yahzee boarded the bus, no one acknowledging him, no nods, no eye contact. He dropped in next to Whitehorse, stuffed his bag beneath the seat in front of him, and looked past his apparently sleeping friend out the open window at his wife and son and the rest of his family, waving at him, receding in the dust as the bus rumbled away from the trading post.

Would he ever see them again? This thought, this terrible thought, hit him like a physical blow. He sat back and felt an emptiness consume him; it was as if his being had been hollowed out. . . .

Then, showing none of this, he turned toward Whitehorse and said, in the language of the People, "I am almost surprised to see you on this bus."

Without opening his eyes, Whitehorse said in the same tongue, "Could I let our white brothers think you were the best we had?"

That made Yahzee smile—a little. He gazed past his friend out the window at Monument Valley, the land he was leaving behind—the land he was offering his life to defend.

Then he saw something he'd missed—boys on ponies, riding bareback, riding hard, pursuing the

bus, coming up alongside, seeing off their warriors, whooping, hollering, like the Indians in the
movies attacking a stagecoach. This too made him
smile—a little—but then the bus outran the boys,
left them behind, as Ben Yahzee and Charlie
Whitehorse and two dozen more Dineeh men
went off to fight the white man's war.

Before long, Yahzee and the others would be
standing, right hands raised, staring solemnly at
the American flag as a white recruiting officer at
Fort Defiance swore them in, taking their oath of
duty to the nation that had conquered and so often
betrayed their ancestors.

Soon Ben Yahzee and Charlie Whitehorse and the
others on their bus joined other Navajo recruits—
many of whom had come by horseback and
wagon—to board trains in Flagstaff for Marine basic training camp at the San Diego Marine Corps
Recruit Depot.

Boot camp—which for the average American
male was a hellish initiation into military life—
did not faze the Dineeh men, who displayed superior agility, endurance and marksmanship.
The Indians embraced the long, brutal days, welcoming calisthentics and marching, excelling at
close-order drill, bayonet training and judo instruction, undaunted by the endless hikes over
rough terrain and breakneck runs over obstacle
courses, unconcerned that infantry training under

combat conditions meant live ammo would whiz over their heads.

What seemed to an average American man a shocking change in living habits and mental attitudes struck these Navajos as reasonable and even enjoyable. Questionable food, irregular hours and damn little privacy presented no particular hardship for a man of traditional ways like Charlie Whitehorse—even for a modern Navajo like Ben Yahzee. Achieving the mental attitude of a warrior was in tune with the outlook passed down to the Dineeh men for generations.

As for Yahzee, he saw the military life as an opportunity, a way to distinguish himself, to show that he and his brothers could perform the duties of a Marine as well as any white man—maybe better.

But Boot Camp and physical challenges were one thing—the duty the two friends were singled out for was something else again, including as it did heavy classroom training. It seemed Yahzee and Whitehorse, having tested well, were among a handful chosen to enter the elite circle known as the codetalkers.

Early in 1942, Philip Johnson—the son of missionaries assigned to the Navajo reservation—approached Major General Clayton Vogel, commander of the Amphibious Corps, Pacific Fleet, to present a new idea for a communications code. The Japanese had broken every previous code and were intercepting critical radio communications, and anticipating every American military move in the Pacific. But Johnson—a rare non-Navajo who spoke their language fluently—believed a code based on the Dineeh's complex, unwritten language, with its unique syntax and tonal qualities, would be unintelligible to the Japanese . . . the one code the Japs could never crack.

Johnson was right: the Navajo Code baffled the best Japanese code breakers, who described the seeming gibberish as a mixture similar to Tibetan and Mongolian.

Of course, Johnson—one of fewer than thirty non-Dineeh speakers of the language on the planet—did not develop the code himself. In the summer of 1942, twenty-nine Navajo recruits went from boot camp in San Diego to the Field Signal Battalion Training Center at Camp Pendleton in Oceanside, California; these men—the first platoon of codetalkers—developed the code themselves, including a dictionary and numerous words given military meanings.

In the oral tradition of the Dineeh, the dictionary and code words were memorized during training. Once you had graduated, your only reference library would be the one between your ears. In addition, codetalkers would take one-hundred-seventy-six hours of basic communciations procedures and equipment instruction, as well as courses in printing and message writing, voice procedure, message transmission, wire laying and pole climbing.

And it was this training—not the rigors of boot camp—that tested the mettle of Charlie White-horse (except for wire laying and pole climbing). Ben Yahzee, on the other hand, was already a skilled student. So sitting in a Camp Pendleton classroom caused Yahzee none of the agony his sheepherder friend suffered.

But if Whitehorse preferred the obstacle course to the classroom, at least the teacher was one of the People: at the front of the class, scrawling with chalk on the blackboard, a veteran codetalker lectured them, pointing out English words and their Navajo equivalents—the sounds of their language given, for the first time, letters in the white man's alphabet. Color illustrations of Japanese planes and tanks were displayed on an easel, for identification and memorization.

Yahzee—hair military short, crisp in his Marine uniform (as were the other Dineeh men around him)—copied the illustrations, making quick, deft sketches in his workbook.

Whitehorse—shorn of his dark flowing locks, just another short-haired man-in-uniform, albeit a big, moon-faced one—peeked over at his friend's handiwork, like a kid cheating on a test.

Ben was adding flourishes to his drawings, inserting Japanese soldiers into the tanks and cockpits . . . and each and every Jap was getting an arrow in the back or a spear in the heart.

Yahzee looked up from his work, caught his friend's eyes, and before Ben could grin in embarrassment, the bigger man bestowed a faint smile, and approving nod.

They may have been students sitting in a classroom, Whitehorse's eyes seemed to say, but they would graduate as fighting men.

3

ON THE WINDWARD (EASTERN) SIDE OF THE ISLAND OF
Oahu, near pineapple fields and banana patches, a
shimmering, far-reaching bay provided an ideal
setting for Kaneohe Naval Air Station. The facil-
ity—well recovered from that fateful attack on December 7, 1941—included landing strips, ramps,
piers, boathouses, repair shops, hangars, offices,
barracks, storehouses, power plant, and radio
center . . . all the operations needed to conduct
modern warfare.

Other operations—the sort that resulted from
modern warfare—were the province of the base
hospital. Under a blue sky, whose white clouds
were so perfectly placed God might have found
work at Metro-Goldwyn-Mayer, were the young

men turned old by war, haunted-eyed sailors and Marines in robes and pajamas, shuffling and strolling, as if in search of something lost, perhaps the occasional arm or leg. Here and there an orderly or a nurse would push dazed, damaged warriors in wheelchairs.

Medicine tray in hand, one of these nurses—Rita Swelton, Des Moines, Iowa—approached one such warrior who sat just off the exercise yard, looking past the archways of the open pale-yellow stucco porch. Behind him, sun filtered in arched windows whose filigree metalwork invoked stained glass, and a cool breeze blew in off the bay.

While Corporal Joe Enders—a brown robe over his tee-shirt and pajama bottoms—indeed sat in a wheelchair, he had all his limbs: one hand covered the sharp, angular features of his face, as he leaned an elbow against the wheelchair's armrest; the other lay limply in his lap as he slouched there. His legs went all the way to the floor, ending in slippers. He was lucky.

Rita was twenty-five, her brown hair so dark it seemed almost black, a slenderly shapely, dark-eyed woman with a fair complexion and a delicately pretty, yet strong, oval face. A Navy nurse, in her white uniform shirt and navy-blue skirt, she moved with grace and efficiency, seemingly all business.

But after seeing that Enders had taken his pills

with the Dixie cup of water, she lingered and set the tray somewhere and pushed his chair out onto the sunshine-dappled grass, chatting with him . . . or was that chattering at him?

"You're better off on the windward side, you know," she said chirpily. "These kids stream into Honolulu, thinking they'll find moonlight and waving palms and sunny beaches and, well, you know . . . pretty girls."

Enders didn't reply.

"Oh, I mean they'll find all those things, only they're going to find other things, too—blackouts and curfews and I'm afraid very limited opportunity to enjoy the moonlight."

Enders was watching another man in a wheelchair—a man with no legs who was staring at nothing.

"I mean, the beaches are crowded, pretty girls are in notorious short supply, maybe one for every hundred men . . . and the training schools and practice maneuvers take up most of a serviceman's time. No, you're lucky to be on the windward side."

A guy on crutches, with one leg, was getting around pretty well, Enders noted.

"You know I have this weekend off, and you're doing so nicely, now. Maybe you could finally get out of here for a few hours. . . . You haven't lived until you've seen the coral gardens through one of those glass-bottomed boats. The water is so crystalline, you can see every detail . . . every little seahorse, and fish of every color. . . . You didn't hear a word I said, did you?"

He looked up; she had edged around, facing him—her arms folded, her expression pretending to be stern.

He almost smiled at her. "You should know by now—you have to talk into my right ear."

She did not smile at him. "I *was* talking into your right ear."

"Oh. Well, I guess I got distracted. Happens when a guy is talking to a good-looking dame."

Arching an eyebrow, she knelt beside him—on his right side. "It also happens when you can't see my mouth."

"It is a nice mouth."

"I'm talking about you reading my lips, Joe."

"I don't have to read your lips. I read you like a book, period."

"Joe. . . ."

He shrugged. "I'm getting better at it."

She sighed, stood. "Let's walk a little."

"Okay."

Leaving the wheelchair behind, she guided him by the arm around the sunny courtyard. She whispered—into his right ear.

"You should go home. You could go home. What kind of man comes back from combat, with a ticket to the mainland, and doesn't use the darn thing?"

Enders did not whisper. "A man who needs to get back into combat."

"Joe . . . Joe, why?"

He stopped and looked at her—right at her. "Rita, I have my reasons. Are you going to help me or not?"

She avoided his gaze. Shaking her head, she said, "You're not going to fool anybody. Who are you trying to kid? You're a mess."

Just then an orderly rolled a gurney past them, bearing a double amputee, who was mumbling deliriously in a heavily medicated fog.

Enders watched the orderly disappear with his cargo into the hospital, and turned to the pretty nurse and said, flatly, "No—*that* guy's a mess."

"Joe . . . how can you be so callous?"

"He *can't* go back—I *have* to."

"Why?"

"Because I have my legs and my arms and I haven't quite lost my mind, yet. I want to go back, Rita. I need to go back. Help me."

She let her air out—it was both sigh and shudder; she looked as though she might cry. "Oh, Joe. . . ."

"Rita, my hearing's gonna return. I just don't want to wait that—"

"Damnit, Joe—you have a perforated left

eardrum." Her mouth tightened to a line, her chin crinkled. "Your equilibrium's shot all to hell. How can you go back to combat if you can't even stand on your own two feet?"

He pulled away from her, and the suddenness of it threw the nurse off balance, in every sense of the phrase; and the corporal took a step, without her—a shaky one, but a step. Then he took another, almost falling to the grass, but keeping his stability nonetheless. When he did falter, he was near enough to a wall to brace himself.

She came to him, took his arm, whispered into his good ear: "Maybe you're right, Joe—maybe your hearing will come back. You'll being walking tightropes before you know it."

"Damn right."

She was almost hugging his arm, now—in a very loving, unprofessional way. "So, in the meantime, stay here on Oahu—somebody's got to keep us WAVEs company, right?"

He looked at her—hard. No lies between them—no manipulation. "Are you going to help me or not?"

But right now Rita wasn't looking at him—she was gazing past him, at an ambulance rolling in to the emergency lane, carrying more of the war's wounded who had to be dealt with.

Enders turned and watched as orderlies emptied these casualties off racks in back of the vehicle, and began hurriedly wheeling the wounded to surgery.

He turned back to the nurse and said, "I'm just takin' up space, baby—what do you say?"

"I have work to do," she said, and brushed past him. She sounded cold, but Enders didn't believe it. She had shown in her eyes that she would help him.

And help him she did.

A white-haired white-coated doctor—so business-like Enders wondered if the guy had ever laughed at anything—stood at his console of dials and switches. This was the gizmo that would decide Enders's fate.

Within the sound-proofed booth, separated by a wall of glass from the doctor and a certain nurse, Joe Enders—free of bandages now, wearing headphones—took the crucial hearing test.

The doctor twisted a treble knob, and Enders raised his right hand. Then the doc twisted a bass knob and Enders pointed down. Doing fine.

But that had been the corporal's right ear. It was his left that could send him back to Philly, and forever off the front lines.

The doctor, an eyebrow raised, said, "A marked improvement, nurse."

In her blue-jacketed uniform, Rita Swelton looked as business-like as the doc, who she stood just behind. Enders could not hear what the doctor said to her—but he could read the man's lips, just as he could read Rita's . . . and her mind.

"But wasn't it the corporal's left ear that suffered the most damage?" the doc asked her.

"That's correct, sir," she said.

Nodding to himself, the doctor twisted the treble knob on the left side of his console.

Enders watched Rita who pointed inconspicuously up with her left thumb.

And Enders, hearing jack shit in his headphones, raised his left hand accordingly.

When the doctor threw a low tone at him, Enders aped the WAVE's signal by pointing down.

The examination continued on like this for some time, and finally the doctor—amazed—turned to Rita, who quickly tucked her hands behind her.

"Damage like this doesn't simply reverse itself," he said.

"Perhaps the initial diagnosis was incorrect," she said.

The doctor frowned at her.

"At any rate, it is a remarkable recovery," she said.

The doc—seeming almost irritated that his patient was doing so well—was making notes, shaking his head unbelievingly . . . but recording what appeared to be the astounding facts of the case.

With the doc's attention on his notes, Enders grinned at Rita and winked at her.

But the nurse did not wink back—her expression was grave, as if the help she had given him were the worst thing she'd ever done, the biggest mistake she'd ever made. . . .

Back in uniform, Corporal Joe Enders sat in the waiting room, cap in his hands, watching the walls, listening to the discordant click-clack music of a rednecked staff sergeant at a nearby desk doing his best to type up paperwork. In a bustling bullpen, other typewriters clattered with more confidence, as files went in and out of file cabinets and notices went up and down on bulletin boards and staffers moved in and out of the clapboard office building. New assignments being made.

One of them would be his.

Just behind the painfully typing staff sergeant, the office door clicked open and a lanky brown-haired sergeant in his late twenties, with boyish, alert features, emerged. Ashen-faced, he looked like he'd been struck a good one in the bread basket.

The young sarge stood there for a moment, framed in the doorway, and stuck his cap on his head—crookedly. The guy looked at Enders, who returned the glance, but the stunned sarge really just looked right through him.

Then the guy stumbled out of the office, into daylight, no clue his cap was on half-assed, distracted as hell.

Enders was wondering what that was about when the staff sergeant looked up from his typing to nod and say, "You're up, mac!"

Enders entered the small office, closing the door behind him, approaching the desk, behind which sat a major, whom Enders saluted.

Major Mellitz was a no-nonsense, crisply uniformed officer with dark hair sitting on a high forehead, and a hard pockmarked face only slightly softened by sky-blue eyes. To one side of his desk stood an American flag; behind him the slats of blinds let in soft sunlight. A ceiling fan stirred the air as the major sat staring at an open file folder, even as he tamped down tobacco in a pipe.

"At ease, Corporal," the major said, without looking up from the file.

Enders did as he was told—but he didn't feel at ease. The major projected a coldness that told Enders at once things were not wonderful. Was Mellitz some sort of USMC hatchet man? From the expression on that young sergeant's face, some kind of boom had been lowered. Had Enders's scam about his "miracle cure" been discovered?

Still without looking at the corporal, the major said, in a mellow, uninterested baritone, "You've done well as a Marine, Corporal."

"Thank you, sir."

"Better than as a civilian, anyway. I don't suppose I have to tell you what's in this file."

"No, sir."

That as a boy Enders had stolen—and crashed—a motorbike. That he'd been kicked out of high school for "attitude problems." That he had been charged with assault and battery before his eighteenth birthday.

Finally the major looked up from the file, mild astonishment on the pockmarked face. "A priest? You beat up a priest?"

Enders risked a shrug. "He was assistant principal at Archbishop Keenan High School, sir. Head disciplinarian. You know how it goes."

"Actually, I don't—public school kid, myself." He sighed, thumbing deeper in Enders's file, getting his pipe going. "You had a few dust-ups in boot, a few minor slips."

"I ribboned in marksmanship, sir."

"I know. It's in here. . . . So is you getting singled out for valor in Shanghai. And you made a hell of a stand on the Canal. . . . I notice you don't wear your Silver Star."

"I choose not to, sir."

"That's your right. Tough piece of real estate, I hear."

"Yes, sir. Pretty tough, sir."

"And after all these months recuperating, you want to jump back in?"

"I do, sir. Very much so."

Smoke coiled from the pipe. "It wouldn't have been hard for you to maneuver your way stateside."

"Very hard, sir. Impossible."

The major was studying him—beautiful blue eyes in a ravaged face. He closed the corporal's file. "I guess you must know that the Japs have pretty much busted every code we've thrown at 'em."

"Yes, sir. Cost a lot of Marine lives, sir."

"You run into any Indians on the Solomons?"

"Indians, sir?"

"Navajos."

"I heard something about that, sir. Communications men?"

"That's right, Corporal. Corps has developed a new code based on the Navajo language. First code the Nips haven't been able to crack—working real good."

"Excellent, sir."

"Making a big impact, matter of fact. So much so, the Navy's decided to go to great lengths to protect that code . . . which is where you come in."

"Me, sir?"

"You. You're going to pair up with one of these . . . codetalkers. You are going to keep his Indian ass safe . . . and the code with it."

"Sir . . . I'm not sure I understand."

"Your job is to keep that Indian alive so he can do his job."

"Begging the major's pardon—but I think I might best serve the Corps by killing Japs, not baby-sitting some Tonto . . . sir."

Major Mellitz sighed pipe smoke; the blade of the fan caught it and it curled upward—like little smoke signals. "Corporal Enders, do you imagine I pulled your name from a hat? You are supposed to be gung ho. Do you or do you not wish to return to combat?"

"I do, sir."

"Good. Fine. Well, we need good Marines for this key assignment, and that is why you're standing here right now. Few jobs you could be given would be more important. You *are* a good Marine, Corporal?"

"Yes, sir."

Mellitz grunted, and handed him a manila envelope. "Have a look."

Enders took the envelope, opened it and shook out the contents: several photographs—grisly ones.

An obviously dead Marine—his body maimed, even mutilated—sat tied with rope to a chair. A victim of torture, the Marine's features had a foreign cast . . . almost Asian, with the same high cheekbones, similar dark complexion.

"That's a Navajo of ours, found like that in a hut on Bouganville," Mellitz said. "We believe he was tortured to death in an attempt by Japanese intelligence to bust our code."

Enders returned the photos to their envelope, placed it on the desk as he said, "How do you know he didn't give it up, sir?"

"That 'Tonto' couldn't have if he wanted to—not every Navajo in the Corps is a codetalker, Corporal."

"I thought the code was the Navajo language, sir."

"No, it's based on their language . . . but it's still a code. Navajos who haven't gone through training call the code 'crazy Navajo.' Sounds like their language, but it's known only to a relative handful of these Indians."

"What would happen if one of the . . . the real codetalkers were captured, sir?"

He drew on his pipe, smiled around the stem—kind of a ghastly smile, at that. "Now you're thinking, Corporal. From what we understand, Tojo would like nothing better than to catch a live one by the toe." The smile disappeared. "Corporal—what I'm about to tell you is not to leave this room."

Uneasy, Enders said, "Understood, sir."

"Ostensibly we are assigning white American bodyguards to codetalkers because these Navajos might be mistaken as Japanese."

"I can see that, sir."

"But there's more to it. . . . These are your orders: you will be assigned to one codetalker. Under no circumstances are you to allow your codetalker to be taken prisoner. The code must not fall into enemy hands—your mission is not to protect the codetalker . . . but the code itself . . . and at all costs."

Enders said nothing, blinking at the pipe smoke sent his way by the blades of the fan churning the air overhead.

Eyebrows lifted high over eyes as blue as the Hawaiian sky. "Is my meaning clear, Sergeant?"

"Uh . . . crystal clear, sir. But it's 'Corporal.' "

"Not now it isn't," Mellitz said. "You just got promoted. . . . Congratulations."

And Sergeant Joe Enders just stood there, never dreaming a promotion would feel like this—like shit—never thinking his efforts to get back into combat, where he might make it up to the men for whose deaths he felt responsible, would result in a homicidal assignment like this.

4

FOR THE NAVAJO CODETALKERS, THE FINAL TRAINING ground was Camp Tarawa near Kamuela on the Big Island of Hawaii. Boot camp and code school behind them, the codetalkers would practice island-storming maneuvers, for the upcoming campaign for the islands of Saipan, Tinian and Okinawa. This part of Hawaii, near the vast Parker Ranch, had historical significance as a jumping-off place—one-hundred-and-fifty years or so ago, King Kamehameha gathered his forces here before setting sail for the invasions of Maui, Molokai and Oahu.

Camp Tarawa was a sprawling Army camp established not long after the attack on Pearl Harbor, initially called Waimea (after a nearby sleepy little town) and then, in December 1943, shifted over for use by the Second Division Marines, just returned from an amphibious assault on the island of Betio in the Tarawa Atoll, combat veterans of which renamed the camp after the battle they'd just survived.

Sprawled in a valley otherwise characterized by windswept sugarcane fields, the tent city of Camp Tarawa provided neat, ordered, spartan living space for the men of the Second Division. In this setting, Ben Yahzee and Charlie Whitehorse would become acquainted with the white men who had been assigned as their bodyguards.

Right now, as a deuce and a half—a two-and-a-half-ton military vehicle—rumbled down the Belt Highway toward that tent city, bearing Yahzee and Whitehorse in its truckbed, morning was working its wonders on the scenic Hawaiian landscape, and Camp Tarawa was just waking up. A few Marines, however, had been up for some time—including the two white sergeants who were assigned to the codetalkers.

Running through Camp Tarawa's exercise area in full 782 Gear, helmets and packs and all, a group of Marines were already at it, having a pre-breakfast outing. Sergeant Peter Anderson was fit enough—a slender but wiry type—but the heavy gear was no picnic. Still, seeing up ahead the Marine he recognized as the corporal who'd followed him into the major's office the other day, Anderson pushed hard, managing to catch up.

Falling in alongside the sturdy, sharp-featured jarhead, Anderson—trying not to huff and puff, and failing—said, "That Mellitz sure is a charmer."

Cool hooded eyes glanced sideways at Anderson, a nonverbal response punctuated by the tiniest of nods.

"Kinda ugly, too," Anderson continued, running along next to the untalkative Marine—who, Anderson noticed, was also a sergeant now. "We could use that bastard in the field . . . scare the Nips to death."

That made the impassive Marine smile a little.

"I'm Pete Anderson, only they call me Ox."

An eyebrow raised over a still hooded eye.

Voice breathy and bouncy as they jogged quickly along, Anderson explained: "Hey, I'm no Charles Atlas, I'll grant you . . . see, I'm from Oxnard—that's north of Hollywood, in California."

"Joe Enders," the Marine said, not missing a step, making Anderson work to keep up. "Philadelphia. . . . That's south of New York. In New York."

He could tell Enders was about as warm as Mellitz; still, the slim Californian pushed himself to stay with the guy; Anderson was crawling with curiosity, wondering if the two of them had pulled the same sorry duty.

Anderson asked, "You been with JASCO long?"

JASCO: Joint Assault Signal Company.

"Naw," Enders said, keeping the pace quick. "Just got my ass outa sick bay—JASCO's where they stuck me."

"Sick bay, huh? Malaria?"

"Some of that. Some of the other, too."

"No shit—took a hit, did ya?"

Enders didn't reply at first; then—reluctantly—he bestowed Anderson a curt nod.

Anderson laughed and grabbed his ass with one hand. "Me, too! Now, when they call me half-assed, they got somethin'!"

That earned Anderson another little smile from Enders.

Hoping he wasn't coming off as a goddamn ear-banger, Anderson nonetheless pressed on with the conversation. "Yeah, fuckin' Jap 7.7—you believe that shit?"

"I believe it."

"Hey, don't think I caught it in the can 'cause I was goin' the wrong way! Fuck, no—little yellow cocksuckers came up behind us. Bad idea on their part—they're with their ancestors, now."

Enders nodded in approval.

"Hell of it is," Anderson admitted, "I thought I'd bought my ticket stateside. Figured it was the million-dollar wound. . . . You know what the chief medic said?"

"No."

" 'We don't do that much sitting in the Marines, son.' "

"He ain't seen combat, that doc."

"Goddamn right. Anyway, soon as I learned to sit on one cheek, these new orders come through. . . ."

No response from Enders, who—like Old Man River—just kept rolling along.

Guts killing him, Anderson said, "Tell me somethin', Joe—you weren't wearin' three stripes when you were sitting out in front of Mellitz's office, were ya?"

Enders gave Anderson another glance. "I didn't think you even saw me. You left with your fuckin' cap on sideways."

"That's 'cause my head was on sideways. . . . That third stripe, it's new, ain't it?"

Enders said nothing.

Anderson patted his arm. "Mine, too—only they coldcocked me . . . promoted me first, then gave me this shit assignment. Your, uh, JASCO duty—anything to do with communications? Radiomen?"

Enders said nothing.

Damn near panting, Anderson managed, "Navajo radiomen, Joe?"

Enders said, "Not at liberty to say."

"Yeah, me too neither. And I bet it's the same goddamn duty I ain't at liberty to tell you about . . . hell of a thing."

Enders swallowed, slowed just a bit, his eyes admitting to Anderson that he, too, had been assigned an Indian—with orders to kill the poor bastard, if need be, to prevent the Japs from getting that precious Navajo code.

"The Marines don't seem to be a democracy, Sergeant," Enders said.

"Yeah—I noticed."

And Enders picked up the pace—really picked it up.

Anderson tried to hold his own, but the somber sergeant from Philly soon left the California boy in his wake. Anderson frowned, shaking his head, his guts burning. The son of a bitch was running like Jesse Owens, boondockers and all—and he was just out of sick bay? Shit.

By mid-morning, sun blazing down, Anderson had caught up to Enders, albeit not in the exercise area; and a wary sort of friendship—born of their dual, dire responsibilities—was growing. The two men sat at the mouth of a tent, Anderson in his tee shirt, Enders bare-chested, disassembling and reassembling their respective Thompson machine guns.

Anderson was good at this—Enders was better.

The process was repeated, again and again, Anderson always a lick behind, in what was as much a ritual of combat as any kind of real preparation. Neither man noticed, at first, as the deuce and a half rolled into Camp Tarawa, bearing a pair of Navajo codetalkers with their radio packs on their backs, where in earlier days—like a few months ago—a quiver of arrows might have been found.

As the truck pulled to a stop in the compound, not far from their tent, the vehicle's squeal of brakes brought Enders's eyes up, while his hands kept working. He watched as the two bronzed Marines climbed down off the truck bed.

"There's the babies we're sitting," Enders said.

Anderson still lost in the Tommy gun ritual, trying to keep up, said, "Huh?"

"Our Indian radiomen."

Anderson lifted his eyes. Shrugged. "Look pretty normal."

"You were expecting war paint?"

Halting his Thompson assembly, Anderson studied the two Navajos, who were just sort of standing there, looking bewildered, as if they'd been deposited on the moon.

"Maybe we oughta go introduce ourselves," Anderson said.

"Anderson?"

"Make it 'Ox,' would you?"

"Anderson?"

He swallowed. "Yeah?"

"Don't get too attached to 'em."

Yahzee and Whitehorse—having watched the truck drive unceremoniously off, leaving them in the dust—were now wheeling slowly around, taking in the tent city, and the compound of quonset huts, with its suburb of obstacle courses in the background.

Everywhere he looked, Yahzee saw a white man—moving quickly. Knowing where he was going.

Whitehorse said, in the Dineeh tongue, "Ever see so many white men?"

"Now we know how Custer felt," Yahzee said.

Yahzee took a deep breath, remembering what one of the seasoned codetalkers had told them at Camp Pendleton: "The white man's world is no longer an adobe of mysterious enemies, but a place where the red man can enter."

A pair of white Marines, laden with rifles and bazookas, were walking by, and Yahzee smiled at them, and said, in his best English, "You fellas know where we might find Second Joint Assault Signal?"

"How the fuck should I know, mac?" one of them said.

"Do I look like your fuckin' mother, shitbird?" the other one growled.

And then were gone.

"Thanks," Yahzee said, still smiling. "Thanks a bunch."

Whitehorse lifted an eyebrow, saying in their native tongue, "That went well."

"Don't take it hard," a voice said in English.

Yahzee and Whitehorse turned and a slim, smiling Marine in his tee shirt and dog tags came ambling up to them.

"That's exactly what they'd have said to me," he said. And he stuck out his hand. "Anderson, Pete Anderson. But my friends call me 'Ox.' Call me Ox."

They shook hands all around.

"Which of you jarheads is Whitehorse?" Anderson asked.

"Charlie Whitehorse," Whitehorse said, pointing to himself.

"Well, Uncle Sam thinks you and me are the next Fred Astaire and Ginger Rogers, and who are we to disagree?"

"I'm okay with that," Whitehorse said. "As long as I'm not Ginger."

Anderson laughed, nodded toward Whitehorse and said to Yahzee, "I like this guy. Is he always this funny?"

"Hilarious," Yahzee said, deadpan. "I'm Ben Yahzee. Who's my dancing partner, d'you know?"

"Yeah, that bundle of joy sitting over there makin' love to his Tommy gun—Joe Enders. From Philly."

"Philly?" Whitehorse asked.

"Philadelphia," Yahzee explained. "City of Brotherly Love."

Anderson flinched a non-smile. "Maybe not in Joe's case."

At the mouth of his tent, a fair distance away,

Enders wasn't hearing much of this—and wasn't trying to, either. He put his reassembled Thompson down and dug out of his khaki trouser pocket his cigarette case—a battered metal affair with the USMC insignia etched in its tarnished skin.

Inside the lid of the case was a picture—a picture of loved ones; Enders was no different than any guy, in that regard, keeping a picture of those he valued. These were not mom and dad and sis and bro, however, or the gal back home or even goddamn Betty Grable. This was a dog-eared snapshot of men who had died on a beach on a godforsaken island.

He selected a cigarette—one of his homerolled, he hated tailormades—and, leaving the case lid up, set fire to the tip of the cig, while he took several long moments staring at the boys who had died because of him.

One of the Indians seemed to be walking toward him—a slender, angular-featured guy in his twenties—and Enders got up and walked away. He had somewhere to go—he just hadn't decided where that was, yet.

All day the sky had been as perfectly blue as Hawaii's reputation had promised; but by late afternoon thunderclouds had rolled in, black as the night that was coming. And by chow time, the rain was pounding Camp Tarawa, slapping at the mess tent's canvas like sarcastic applause.

As Marines scurried with their trays to find shelter wherever they could, Joe Enders didn't bother. Some battles you couldn't win, and the rain would prevail here; hell, he was already soaked to the skin—still, he liked—if "liked" was the word—his shit-on-a-shingle dry.

So, as he sat perched on the running board of an armored vehicle, a half-track, with the little tin tray in his lap, he used one hand to hold his helmet over the lumpy pile of creamed-beef that had been plopped onto the burnt toast, keeping the food away from the pelting rain. Using a salt shaker he'd pilfered from the mess tent, he used his free hand to salt the hell out of the SOS. It was salty already, but his taste buds had seemed dulled, ever since the Canal. What would have pursed the lips of an average man seemed a tad more palatable now to Enders.

Suddenly the rain seemed to stop, or anyway none was touching him, though the sound of thunder and lashing storm continued. Somebody was standing next to him, blocking the rain, but also intruding on his privacy.

Enders looked up at the young, sturdy, oval-faced Indian. Christ, his eyes were black—like a fucking shark.

But at least his smile was white, in the bronze face. The Indian, who was standing there getting drenched, trying to lean over his tray to protect his own food, said, "Name's Ben. Ben Yahzee."

Enders met the man's gaze, kept chewing his mouthful of SOS.

"The Corps paired us up," the Indian said. "How are you doing?"

Enders returned his attention to his plate, speared a forkful of unappetizing goo, meat and toast, inserted the stuff in his mouth, and chewed.

The Indian's smile faded, but he kept at it, nodding out at the rain slanting down on the compound. "Recruiting officer at Fort Defiance told us Hawaii was heaven on earth. . . . Guess he spoke with forked tongue."

Enders said nothing. Chewed.

The Indian asked, "Mind if I join you?"

Enders didn't say no.

The Indian sat on the running board next to Enders. Looking down at his food, which—like him—was getting sopped in the rain, Yahzee asked, "What the hell is this crap?"

"SOS," Enders said.

"Isn't that a distress signal?"

"Shit on a shingle. Corps calls it chow."

"That's the best wartime propaganda yet." Yahzee took a bite; rain battered the half-track like unrelenting machine-gun fire. "Sergeant Anderson says you're from Philly. Birthplace of the nation, liberty bell, Ben Franklin and all that."

"Yeah. All that."

The Indian studied Enders for a moment,

watched how the seasoned Marine kept his helmet over his food, and said, "That's one way to keep your chow dry."

Enders said nothing as the Indian began awkwardly removing his helmet, holding the tray of food in one hand, fumbling at the leather strap with the other. The juggling act quickly went south, as Yahzee lost his grip on the food tray, and almost dropped it, recovering it at the last moment . . .

. . . but bumping into Enders in the process, knocking the sergeant's tray out of his grasp and onto the muddy ground. Rain beat on the upside-down tray like a little drummer boy. Enders turned to the Indian and gave him a long, unblinking look.

"Oh shit," the Indian said, "I'm sorry! I'm a clumsy fool. . . ."

"What's your name again, Private?"

"Yahzee. Ben Yahzee."

"Ever see any combat? Some of you boys were on the Island."

"The Island?"

"Guadalcanal."

"I, uh . . . no, this is my first tour."

"Cruise."

"What?"

"We call it a cruise, not a tour of duty."

Rain streamed down the Indian's face like tears. "Just because I haven't seen any combat. . . . I gotta say I'm sure looking forward to it."

"To combat?"

"Yes, sir."

"Don't call me 'sir,' Private."

"Sorry, Sergeant. But I am."

"You are what?"

"Looking forward to getting into combat."

"Are you now."

And Enders took the salt shaker out of his pocket and began to douse Yahzee's plate of SOS with it.

"Thanks," Yahzee said. "But, uh . . . whoa! That's enough."

Enders kept salting the food, though, and Yahzee said nothing more. Finally the sergeant stopped, put the shaker away, and plucked the tin plate from the Indian's one-handed grasp, leaving him sheltering an empty lap with his helmet.

And Enders, cradling his helmet over the Indian's chow, walked off with it, in search of a new place to eat in quiet.

Several moments later, Charlie Whitehorse joined his friend Ben Yahzee, who was sitting on the half-track running board in the rain. Whitehorse sat next to Yahzee, in the spot that had been Enders's, and began eating, making no effort to keep the raindrops from watering down his creamed beef.

In the Dineeh language, Whitehorse asked, "What is your white man like?"

Yahzee was watching Enders moving down between rows of tents, protecting the food with his helmet. Whitehorse, noticing the spilled tray, tossed his friend a damp biscuit.

"Salty," Yahzee said in English.

And took a bite of biscuit.

5

THE SKY GOT THE RAIN OUT OF ITS SYSTEM, BUT THE MEMory of moisture hung in the humid, cigarette-smoke-laden air within the dusty-floored tent where the men of Second Recon were billeted, marking time till they were shipped out. A poker game was in progress, a footlocker turned into an altar of coins and dollars and playing cards.

Anderson was dealing seven card stud, eyes slitted, smiling like a joker, passing out cards and commentary with ease. "Pair of cowboys for our man Joe to ride—don't get your ass stuck by that suicide king, now."

Enders grunted.

John Nells, Providence, Rhode Island—a handsome kid with a flat nose, sensitive mouth and a propensity for worrying about the new bride he'd left behind—asked nobody in particular, "What's a suicide king?"

Ronald "Harry" Harrigan, Daytona Beach, Florida, a blue-eyed, good-natured All-American boy who'd brought a tan and sunbleached blonde hair along with him to the war, said, cigarette bobbling, "*That's* a suicide king, Nellie—king of hearts."

"I still don't get it," Nells said.

"Possible straight for the Greek," Anderson said.

Watching his latest club arrive, Nicolas Pappas, Trenton, New Jersey—dark-haired, dark-eyed, olive-skinned, with a winning smile and a cynical outlook—said, "Whoa, Nellie—can't you see the son of a bitch is sticking a sword through his own head?"

"More shit for Rhode Island," Anderson said, tossing Nells his card.

Nells, possibly shaken by the suicide king explanation, folded up. "This ain't gettin' better."

"Jesus, ya little girl—nobody even bet yet," drawled Charles Rogers of Dallas, Texas—"Chick" to his buddies—spitting tobacco juice into a sardine tin. Chick's disgust seemed a little suspect, since he'd folded the round before. He shook his head, sighed. "Shit, man, what are we doin', sittin' here with our thumbs up our butts—when we are gettin' *into* this thing?"

Enders, sitting with a poker face carved out of stone, said, "Careful what you wish for."

Anderson tossed a card onto Harrigan's hand. "Not sure what you're buildin' there, Tarzan. . . . And a third nine for the dealer, 'cause a man simply has to be good to himself."

Various grunted obscenities greeted that remark, which only made Anderson's grin grow wider.

In tee shirts and dogtags, everybody was sitting like Indians, except Yahzee and Whitehorse, who were not in the game, taking up the lower and upper berths respectively of a nearby bunk bed. Yahzee was writing his wife, his penmanship precise, neat; above him, Whitehorse had his hands behind his head, elbows winged out, as he stared up at the tented ceiling.

Eyeing his hole cards, Harrigan tossed a quarter out. "Don't judge a book by its cover," he said, referring to the nondescript hand he had showing. Then he turned to the Texan and said, "I got a buddy in Intelligence says we're shipping out soon."

"How soon?" Nells asked, not quite hiding his alarm.

"Next week."

Chick blew a Texas version of a Bronx cheer. " 'Next week'—I been hearin' 'next week' for a month of next weeks."

Nells managed a smile. "I wouldn't care if it was next year."

Enders, Pappas, Harrigan and Anderson all stayed in; the pot was right.

Pappas was eyeing Harrigan, studying him, trying to sort the big talk from the inside dope. "You really got a friend in Intelligence, Harry?"

Anderson glanced over the top of his cards. "Military intelligence—you heard what that is, ain't ya? Contradiction in terms."

Harrigan said to Pappas, "Hey, Pappy—I got friends everywhere, you know that."

Enders turned over his hole cards. "Can your friends beat kings over queens? Read 'em and weep, ladies."

The full house—all kings and queens in royal array—was a lovely thing to see. Anderson, losing with his three nines, could admire it even when someone else benefited. Others took it less well.

"Fuck this shit!" Pappas said, standing. Heading for his bunk, he said, "I think if I saw you rake one more pot in, Enders, I'd bust out crying."

"Thanks for sparing us," Enders said, coolly separating quarters, dimes and nickels, fashioning them into neat little towers.

Nells, who'd been doing respectably, eyed his holdings, twisting his wedding ring anxiously. "I'm about even—think I'll call it quits myself, maybe write the little lady."

"Letter a day keeps the milkman at bay," Chick said.

That got a laugh from everybody, including a nervous one from Nells, who headed for his rack.

This left Anderson, Rogers, Harrigan and Enders.

Enders was shuffling, while Anderson called over to the bunk where the two Navajos were stretched out. "We could use a little new blood in this game—you gents interested?"

Chick, seeing who Anderson was inviting, smirked and picked up a card and held it in front of his forehead. "Oh, yeah, sure—then we can play Indian poker!"

But this time nobody laughed—except Chick, of course, who was cackling at his own wit. From the top bunk, Whitehorse turned his head and his eyes were hard and glittering in the cigarette-smoke haze.

"No Indian poker at this table," Anderson said, as if Chick's proposal of that silly game—in which a single card was held up so that a player could see everyone's card but his own—had been serious, and not just a racial insult. "No 'Man or Mouse,' either, or fuckin' wild cards. . . . Ben? Charlie? Play if you want."

Yahzee, half-sitting, leaning on an elbow, seemed hesitant.

Enders stopped shuffling. "For Christ sake, yes or no? I gotta deal before the spots wear off."

Yahzee scrawled a close to his letter—"Miss you, love you. Kiss little George for me." Then he folded the sheet of paper and swung off the bunk, headed over.

"Deal me in," he said. "And keep your wallets handy."

Anderson remained impressed with how well these Indians spoke—no accent, really, except a measured, quietly musical quality that should have seemed stilted but didn't.

"Don't dream you're gonna scalp *me*, Chief," Chick snorted, while Yahzee squeezed in between Anderson and Enders, avoiding the Texan.

Enders began to deal the cards vertical and crossways, on the middle of the footlocker. "Game's called Fiery Cross, boys. A travelling sales-man named McRoberts taught it to me—high low, hoggers okay, and the ace goes both ways . . . like Chick, here."

"Very funny," the Texan said, lighting up a fresh cigarette.

"I thought we were gonna play poker," Yahzee said.

Enders shrugged. "Dealer's choice."

"Ah," Anderson said, "he's just showin' off. If you ever played a high-low game, this is like any other. . . . Which is to say, a goddamn waste of time and money."

Whitehorse was climbing down off his bunk.

"Room here for you, too, Charlie," Anderson said, "next hand."

Whitehorse shook his head, and went outside. He was carrying something, but Anderson couldn't quite make out what.

Enders was answering a few questions about the game while Anderson watched his Navajo, who began playing a musical instrument, a wooden, five-fingered affair about a foot long—obviously, a Navajo variation on a flute.

Whitehorse began to play, and the sound was deep-throated and haunting.

"Unusual," Anderson said, as the strange, strangely lovely strains provided an ethereal backdrop for their smoky game.

"Benny Goodman's got nothin' to worry about," Chick said. "What the hell you waitin' for, Ox? Ante up! You, too, Chief."

Yahzee tossed in his dime, then said to Enders, "You know how Chick knows I'm a chief, don't you?"

"Not a clue," Enders said.

Yahzee grinned and looked from face to face, except the Texan's. "He watches me showering in my war bonnet."

Chick squinted at this, but the others laughed—except for the Texan, of course . . . and Enders.

"Can we just play?" he asked. "If I wanted comedy, I'd listen to Bob the fuck Hope."

The edge in Enders's voice turned the play serious, quiet . . . quiet except for the haunting tune of the Navajo flute, which somehow erased Camp Tarawa in Anderson's mind, replacing it with Southwestern vistas.

The reveille bugle was a far cry from Whitehorse's native flute, but it served to stir Camp Tarawa on a sunny morning that was already working on drying up the puddles from yesterday's storm. As the bugler announced another day, a color guard below unfolded the crisp, clean red-white-and-blue flag, and sent Old Glory flapping into the sun-streaked blue Hawaiian sky. It was about as majestic as this city of tents and quonset huts got.

Nothing ceremonial attached itself to the mid-morning briefing in the cramped tin box of the command shack, in which the men of the Second Recon sat and stood in khaki shirts and trousers, jammed into the limited space, sharing the sticky air as a ceiling fan worked overtime, churning like a prop that couldn't quite get a plane off the ground.

The man in charge—Gunnery Sergeant Eric Hjelmstad—was in his thirties, tall and loose-limbed, brown-haired with a high forehead, cleft chin and craggily pleasant-featured, wind-burnt face. He stood before them, casual and yet clearly in command, speaking with a Norwegian accent that half a lifetime in the States had done little to lessen. He had just told the two dozen men in the sweltering shack that their orders had finally come through.

"Wherever the hell we wind up, you can bet Recon'll be out in front, showin' the Corps the way. . . . I'll be headin' up the second squad, then." He said "then" like "den," and his "the" was almost "de."

Ben Yahzee was paying close attention, but he kept stealing glances at Enders, who was perched on the edge of a desk; the sergeant had a glazed expression, and his shoulders were slumped—almost as if he were being disrespectful of the gunnery sergeant.

"Sergeant Fortino here," Hjelmstad was saying, gesturing to the dark-haired, battle-weary squad leader, "will be in charge of the first."

Fortino, his expression morose, was leaning on his M-1; he gave a half-hearted nod to the men, content to let Hjelmstad do the talking.

"Our job is to sniff out enemy positions, and radio back locations. That's why these new faces are brightenin' up our ranks—JASCO sent over these codetalkers . . . Privates Whitehorse and Yahzee. Welcome to Recon."

The two Indians nodded to the men of the unit, who turned to look them over, getting few nods back.

"We also got a couple of freshly striped sergeants," Hjelmstad said, gesturing to Enders and Anderson, "who'll be coverin' our codetalkers' valuable backsides."

The Texan, Chick, was taking that in—seemingly trying to process the notion of white men protecting red men. He spit tobacco juice.

"We're not gonna be lookin' for a fight," Hjelmstad said. "Recon ain't about playin' hero—it's about gatherin' intelligence, and our codetalkers will help us send back what we find. . . . But Saipan is crawlin' with Japs, you know, who won't give us a warm reception—well, that's wrong, then. It'll be hotter than hell, their reception. . . ."

He said "their" like "dere." Yahzee had never heard such an accent before, and found it fascinating. The men around him, however, seemed less impressed—Pappas, scratching his balls; Nellie, lost in thought, fiddling with his gold band; Harrigan, looking so blond and healthy and yet chain-smoking, even during the lecture. . . .

Then Yahzee returned his gaze to his bodyguard, who seemed not at all to be listening to the gunnery sergeant's briefing—Enders sat perfectly still, sweat trailing down his face in rivulets. Eyes glazed, Enders had his neck back, and was staring up at the ceiling fan, as if he couldn't keep his eyes off the droning thing, as its blades spun 'round and 'round.

What Yahzee could not know was that Joe Enders's bad ear was nearest Hjelmstad, and the gunnery's voice had flattened into a meaningless melange of Norwegian-accented syllables, while the roiling drone of the ceiling fan was filling Enders's good ear, to where he found himself compelled to focus on the mechanical sound of the chopping blades . . .

. . . *And inside his head, Joe Enders heard the harsh chatter of machine guns and the bass drum pounding of artillery and the shrill, shocked cries and screams of dying men, Marines, his friends, cursing him, damning him, goddamn you Joe Enders, goddamn you.* . . .

Enders lurched off the edge of the desk onto unsteady feet. The gunnery sergeant did not lose a beat in his briefing, though he—and all of them— were aware that the JASCO sergeant from Philly was staggering toward the door like a damn drunk. To Enders, the faces of the men of the Second Recon were spinning like they were pasted on those fucking fan blades. Tripping over Yahzee's feet, Enders stumbled toward the door, pushed it open, pitched himself outside.

Yahzee—stunned by the ashen-faced sight of the seemingly impervious Enders reduced to a wreck—stared after his bodyguard, unsure of what . . . if anything . . . he should do. He looked toward Whitehorse for guidance, but Charlie was merely staring dumbfounded where Enders had exited, himself.

Finally Hjelmstad nodded at Yahzee, who was sitting on the edge of his chair, giving him permission, and before long the Indian was moving carefully through Camp Tarawa's head, footsteps echoing off cement within the quonset hut with its crude plumbing, its exposed crappers, the long urinal trough.

On his knees praying to one of the porcelain gods was Joe Enders, puking his guts out.

Yahzee kept a respectful distance, until the retching subsided, then stepped forward and said, his voice hollow in the head, "Don't die on me."

Enders, breathing hard, hair wet with sweat, face as pale as the porcelain, slowly turned and stared at Yahzee with a terrible blankness.

Yahzee dug a roll of Lifesavers from his pocket, holding it out to Enders. "Take one. Helps get rid of the taste. Charlie and me spent most of the boat ride from San Diego hanging over the side."

Enders was just looking at the hand offering the colorful candy, as if inspecting a strange variety of plant.

"You know," Yahzee said, really trying, "not too many bodies of water in Arizona. . . . Lifesavers really helped. Try one."

Sitting on the cement, leaning an arm against the toilet bowl, still breathing hard, Enders said, "What the hell are you doing here?"

"Just, you know . . . trying to help."

"I don't mean that. What are you doing in that uniform?"

Yahzee felt the smile on his face freeze, and a familiar sense of cold rage toward the white man's bigotry began to spread through him, like water seeping into hard earth.

In the meantime, Enders was getting to his feet, making his wobbly way past the Indian to a sink where he turned on the faucet and splashed cold water on his face. Yahzee looked at the man in the mirror—both men in the mirror, actually.

"Why is a red man in the white man's Marines?" Yahzee asked. "It's my country, too, Sergeant. And my war. Like you, I'm fighting for my country and my land. I'm fighting for my people."

"I bet you would fight for your people—I just don't see any of 'em around here . . . besides you and what's-his-name."

"His name is Charlie Whitehorse. Listen, Enders— I'm a codetalker. I have training that no white man is capable of; in two and a half minutes, I can do what used to take your boys four hours. Somebody wearing a lot more stripes than you thinks that's worth something."

Enders looked the slim-waisted Indian up and down. "I'll get my stopwatch out and time you, when the bullets start flying."

Yahzee shook his head. "What the hell is wrong with you?"

And Ben Yahzee, tired of fighting this particular battle, strode out of there, leaving Enders leaning over the sink with nothing to look at but himself.

What Enders saw was a pale, drawn reflection with a dark edge in his bloodshot eyes. He sighed and shook it off and returned to the tin shack for the rest of the briefing.

That evening, on steadier legs, Enders made his way to the rocks that faced the ocean, and stared out at the purple, star-flung Hawaiian sky. He got out a homerolled from his tarnished metal cigarette case—not looking at the picture in the lid—and stared at the night and smoked his cigarette. Harmonica music—melancholy, as if played by some damned soul on death row—floated from the barracks tent.

Enders was not, after all, the only Marine, that night, dealing with private thoughts, concerns, fears. Peter "Ox" Anderson lay on his bunk, playing his sad harmonica, lost in memories of home. Charlie Whitehorse used a whetstone to sharpen his eight inches of bone-handled buck-knife, which lived in a sheath on his left ankle. Nells wrote his daily letter home, stroking the gold band when he searched for words. Pappas had a pile of paper bags which, for his own reasons, he was creasing and then stacking, stuffing them in his pack. Harrigan was a kid playing with matches—flicking them off a matchbook, watching them ignite, fly through the air, only to die in a well-placed bucket of water.

And Ben Yahzee was carefully tucking a picture of his wife and son in the webbing inside his helmet.

As for Joe Enders, he inhaled a last drag on the homerolled and pitched it into the sea, watching its sparking trail disappear into the night.

Then he went in to try to get some sleep, hoping to hell his dreams weren't of combat . . . knowing they would be.

6

CAMP TARAWA TOOK UP FIFTY-THOUSAND ACRES OF THE Parker Ranch, in the lofty saddle of the massive volcanoes of Mauna Kea and Mauna Loa. Second in size only to the King Ranch in Texas, the Parker spread was owned by one Richard Smart—a Parker on the maternal side—who had no interest in ranching. A tall, good-looking man, he had gone to Hollywood, made a minor success before his cover was blown, and now—content to allow others to maintain his property—he sang in nightclubs.

Smart had been patriotic enough to welcome Camp Tarawa to his property, and a more generous, genial host could not be imagined. On the night before the morning Second Recon (and others) would ship out, the sole heir to the Parker fortune threw a beach bash for his Marine and Naval guests, including a combo recruited from the Royal Hawaiian hotel (with Richard Smart as guest vocalist, doing Tin Pan Alley–style island music), a half dozen hula dancers, an outdoor bar and a roaring bonfire.

Under the purple sky and a silver moon and twice as many stars as the heavens could possibly have held, the Marines—with the help of beer, hard liquor and Hawaiian music—were enjoying the hell out of the luau, oblivious to the horrors of wars that soon awaited them on less welcoming tropical isles.

Right now their host was singing "Sweet Leilani," and doing a nice Crosbyesque job of it; but what the leathernecks really appreciated was that—with military approval—Smart had brought a boatload of pretty WAVEs over from Oahu.

On the outskirts of the gathering, down a ways from the orange glow of the bonfire, a trio of WAVEs sat, while several sailors made fools of themselves, flirting drunkenly. Two of the young women endured this, patriotically, but the third—one Rita Swelton—had her eyes fixed on a certain Marine who sat at the outdoor, thatched-hut-style bar, slumped on his stool, an elbow leaned against the counter. She wondered if he had even noticed her.

Joe Enders accepted a fresh glass of Budweiser from a burly native bartender in an aloha shirt that few of the men on the beach could have dared to look at tomorrow morning. But this was tonight, and Enders nodded appreciatively to the bright human beach ball and took a deep swig of the suds.

Then Enders glanced back at the bench where Rita had been sitting and saw two of the WAVEs, paired up with sailors. Disappointed, he was slowly scanning the festivities along the beach for Rita when somebody said something into his left ear—which he of course couldn't quite make out.

He turned and the lovely oval face of Rita Swelton was standing there, looking right at him. Pretty but proper in her blue uniform jacket, her dark eyes flashing, her mouth twitched with amusement as she said, "I said—how's the ear?"

"Perfect," Enders said. "Ideal for hearing only what you want to hear."

He gestured to the stool next to him and she sat. A mild breeze over the ocean fluffed her dark brown hair.

She said, "Somehow I think you were always good at that, even before the damage. . . ." Rather surreptitiously, she got into her black patent leather purse, fished out a bottle of pills, slipped them to him.

Enders allowed his hand to close over the vial,

but his voice was skeptical. "I didn't know nurses prescribed medication."

"Don't you think I know what makes you feel better?"

He smiled just a little.

"Anyway," she said, softly, "if that ear starts aching, take a couple of those—they'll cut the pain but you'll stay nice and alert."

He nodded. "Two . . . and call you in the morning?"

She studied him, seemed to sense that something was different about him. "I don't think so . . . 'cause you won't be here in the morning, will you, Joe?"

"Loose lips."

"Sink ships, yes, I've seen the poster. . . . So you were going to ship out without even buying me a drink."

He gave her half a smirk. "Oughta be ashamed of yourself, hustling servicemen. . . . I saw you with those sailors over there. Don't you know the kind of diseases you can catch from those gobs?"

She flashed him a mock wicked smile. "Where do you think they catch those diseases?"

He laughed, and the sound of it surprised him—it had been just a small laugh, a little laugh . . . but the first one in a long, long time.

"So—what's your pizen?" he asked her.

She twitched another smile. "We might as well

go all out—I'm too dainty and ladylike for a beer.
How about rum?"

"What, something with fruit and umbrellas?"

"No—just rum."

Enders shrugged. "Eddy! Shot of Bacardi."

The burly bartender selected a bottle, and Rita
called to the gaudy-shirted native over some swing
music emanating from the little combo on the
beach. They had gone from "Blue Hawaii" to a
frantic "Sing Sing Sing," difficult for a small combo
to pull off—in fact, impossible. But Ox Anderson
was sitting in on drums and his driving rhythm
was getting the crowd going.

Over this hubbub, Rita yelled to the bartender,
"Make that two!" She turned to Enders. "You *will*
join me?"

"Why not." He swivelled to watch in mild amusement as Anderson enthusiastically beat the hell
out of the drum kit; Enders was relieved that there
was no room for the drums in Ox's ditty bag . . .
that harmonica was bad enough.

Rita lifted her shot glass and said, "Here's to
war."

The sight of her forced, bitter smile gave him a
terrible pang, but he hoisted his shot glass and
joined her in the toast. Then they both threw the
shots back, though Rita's grand gesture collapsed
as, wincing, she had to douse the fire with a swig
of Enders's beer.

"That's what I get for showing off," she said, fanning her face with a red-nailed hand.

The crowd on the beach, still responding to Anderson's drumming, was getting louder—and dumber.

"It's getting a little drunk out," she said.

"I noticed."

Leaning close to his good ear, she whispered, "Get me out of here."

She was still close to him, his beer in her hand, when he said, "I don't think that's such a good idea."

"Why?"

"Liberty secures at midnight."

"It's just nine o'clock, Joe. Why don't we go for a drive?"

"What would we use for a car?"

"Our host provided us girls with wheels. . . . The boat doesn't take us back till the witching hour. And I have the keys."

"Really."

"It's a convertible, Joe."

"Is it?"

"Are you going to make a girl beg?"

"I might."

"Heck with you, then."

"Such language."

She hopped off the stool. "Well, *I'm* going for a drive."

"Room for a passenger?"

"Perhaps. Perhaps." Then she held out her hand, ready for him to lead her from the bar.

Which, as the noise on the beach grew, he did, and soon they were enjoying softer sounds on the sands, as waves crashed in onto the beach, with exploding power that dissipated in soft whispers. The Ford convertible (God bless Richard Smart) was parked at the edge of the wet sand, ashimmer with pale silver moonlight.

Enders, sitting on the passenger side, looked beyond the white breakers toward the darkness, the blackness, of the sea that stretched to seeming infinity. Rita, behind the wheel, sat leaning back, staring at the purple sky and its millions of stars.

Her voice was tiny, childlike, as she said, "Star light, star bright, first star I see tonight. . . ."

"That's the first star you saw tonight?"

"Must you be a killjoy?" She closed her eyes. After a while the lids peeked open, the eyes turned slyly toward him. "Aren't you curious?"

"About what?"

"What I wished for."

"Why do I have the feeling you're gonna tell me anyway?"

"Well, it must not have worked."

"What didn't?"

"See, I wished for you not to be such a horse's patoot."

That made him laugh, and they both liked the sound of it—especially Rita, who slid over, lifting his arm like a lever and sliding under it, snuggling.

"You're a little bold," he said.

"Do you mind?"

"Did I say I did?"

"You know what? I'm going to write you, Joe. And you know what else? You're going to write me back."

"I don't know about that, Rita—they sometimes don't ship letters out from . . . you know."

"Top secret stuff, huh? Well, if they do let you. . . ."

"I'm not much of a letter-writer."

"I'm not gonna check your grammar." She flicked his left earlobe. "You owe me . . . remember?"

He remembered.

"You have to admit . . ." And she gestured to the sea and the surf, the sky and the stars. ". . . this is a beautiful night."

He nodded.

She seemed to sense his unease, but even as her voice tried to stay light, a certain edge crept in. "Maybe you've forgotten, Joe . . . but the world can be a wonderful place."

". . . Not where I'm going."

The conversation had lost its brittle fun. He found himself staring at the blackness of the sea, and the roar of the surf recalled the din of battle, and it seemed suddenly wrong, somehow, to be sitting here in paradise next to this sweet wonderful silly girl . . . damn near sinful.

He didn't know how cold his voice sounded when he said, "Maybe we should get the hell out of here."

She blinked, the only indication of hurt in her pale, pretty face. "Why, Joe?"

"I don't know. Maybe we just should."

"You're right," she said, her voice flaring with irritation. "I mean, Jesus Christ, we wouldn't want to have a good time or anything."

She drew away from him and tried to start the car, the engine refusing to catch; she tried again with the same grinding lack of success. Finally the motor caught, firing to life, and Rita was just about to get it in gear when Enders—watching the angry young woman awash in silver starlight—touched her arm, and when she turned to look at him, he kissed her.

The kiss had urgency in it, and insistence, and she met it with passion.

"Oh, Joe," she said, and in those two words conveyed what they—like so many in their situation before them (and after)—had known: this might be the only night they would ever have.

They undressed each other tenderly, and what they did after that was between them and the surf and the stars and a night that had gone very quiet, an ocean no longer roaring, just whispering, whispering.

Shouts resounded across the bustle of Camp Tarawa, alive with activity the next morning, as the Marines of Second Recon awaited the transports that would deliver them to battle.

Most of these kids had not been in combat before, Enders knew, and he should not be disgusted by their high school team-spirit camaraderie. But something jarred him—the déjà vu of it, the realization that he'd lived this moment before—when blond-headed Harrigan, Pentax in hand, decided to round everybody up for a picture, before they hit the boats.

Herding the men in their full packs took some cajoling, and Harrigan had to promise them all a print, and soon a crooked line of them had formed, including Yahzee and most of the others. Harrigan, cigarette bobbling as he readied the camera, looked around for the missing few, and spotted one: Enders, sitting on his pack, obviously aware of—and ignoring—the group photo.

"Come on, Joe! Squeeze in, here, next to your codetalker."

"I'll pass," Enders said, lighting up a homerolled.

Harrigan seemed about to push the issue, but Enders glared at him, and that ended it. Then the Florida photog coached his models and did his best to focus, making them bunch tighter together.

At Enders's left, somebody said something. He turned and the other Indian, moon-faced Charlie Whitehorse, stood looming over him.

"I said," Whitehorse said, "I don't like pictures, either."

"Yeah? Afraid your spirit'll get captured or somethin'?"

"Naw." He shook his big head. "They never turn out as pretty as I think I am."

In spite of himself, Enders cracked a tiny smile.

Whitehorse was watching Yahzee, hamming it up with the other guys, Pappas and Nellie and Chick, everybody all grins and rabbit ears as the camera started clicking.

"Now my friend there," Whitehorse said, "he looks good in pictures . . . like Gary Cooper. In real life, well. . . ."

Enders and Whitehorse had never had a conversation, really didn't know each other at all. And the look Enders shot the Indian said as much.

"Ben's a good guy," Whitehorse said, in his measured, quietly musical way. "We grew up different. . . . I taught him to ride horses, he taught me to drive a car. I'm what you call traditional, he's modern. But we're friends. Known each other a long, long time."

Enders said, "Is there a point?"

"The point is—take care of him."

Enders exhaled smoke. "That's my orders, Private."

"Good. You just remember that . . . Sergeant."

The eyes of these two hard men locked and, for a moment, Enders felt the chill of menace. Then Whitehorse's stony, damn near sinister countenance dissolved into something friendly as he headed over to the photo shoot, which was wrapping up.

"Hey, how about one more?" Whitehorse said. "Get one of me and my handsome friend."

Harrigan obliged. Then he turned to Enders. "Last chance, Joe—something for your girlfriend!"

Enders shook his head, pitched his cigarette, and took a walk. The only companionship he wanted right now was Rita Swelton's, and she was back in Oahu—and he would soon be on his way to hell.

7

THE FIRST OBJECTIVE IN SECURING THE MARIANAS ISLANDS, Saipan ranked as the highest priority for the American military in the Pacific. The Air Force was anxious to start construction of airfields big enough to hold B-29s, an effort that—once the island was in U.S. hands—would be under way even as assault forces headed for Tinian and Guam.

Two Marine divisions—the Second and the Fourth—would invade Saipan, with the Twenty-seventh Army Division as their back-up. The leathernecks would hit the invasion beaches and push inland, cutting the island in half, and swing around to squeeze the enemy into the north of the island, to contain and then eliminate them. The brass believed Saipan could be captured in a week, freeing up the same forces to jump on to the island of Tinian. But they severely misjudged the numbers and resilience of the Japanese garrison on Saipan, and knew nothing of the island's rugged terrain.

Japanese General Saito positioned his mortars and artillery to deliver death to the landing beaches, with his troops lying in wait for the survivors in well-constructed, heavily fortified positions in the island's interior, taking full advantage of Saipan's tropical landscape. Snipers watched natural avenues of advance; caves were carved into the rocky hills; and spider holes—small foxholes with camouflaged lids—were dug in the vine-choked, grassy earth, and manned by riflemen.

Just before dawn on the morning of June 15, 1944, Marine assault troops dropped from transports onto their assault crafts, which then made their run toward the island, north of the actual landing areas. Naval support ships bombarded the Japanese positions, followed by waves of planes from the escort carriers, soaring low to strafe and bomb the enemy.

The Second Marine Division made up the northern portion of the attack force. The men of Second Recon would be part of the regiment that followed, later that day: though they would soon be out in front of the rest, the Second Recon's role made them too important to be a part of the first waves, who—starting at 0812—headed toward the beaches in their small boats under Hellcat escort.

The pre-landing bombardment of the Japanese positions, however, did not prevent General Saito's men from inflicting incredible damage: in the first half hour, particularly, the Marines racked up extensive casualties. The beaches were strewn with wounded and dead and dying Marines, and flame-consumed landing craft; and the inland attack soon stalled under the pressures of devastating artillery fire and tropical terrain. When the Marines settled in that night, they had made it barely halfway to their day's objective, the line of ridges and hills inland from the beaches . . .

. . . the territory that Second Recon—and specifically the Navajo codetalkers and their American "bodyguards"—would scout.

The morning of the 16th found the Marines on the move.

Surrounded by mountains, Sherman tanks barrelled over the rocky earth, the grinding of their massive gears and the roar of their big engines all but lost in the manic gunfire and earth-jarring explosions. Coming up behind these lumbering mechanical beasts, hundreds of Marines charged up the scraggy slopes, firing as they ran, assaulting the Japanese positions on the hillside.

Streaking overhead were a pair of Hellcat

fighter planes, taking their own crack at the Jap positions, their .50 caliber machine guns spitting hot lead, tearing up the earth and the rocks and the enemy.

But at the same time, machine-gun, mortar and cannon fire from the enemy—in fortified trench lines cut into the top of a ridge—was showering down at the advancing Marines, chewing up flesh, creating screams that cut across engine roar and even explosions, blossoms of blood splashing color on the drab rocky incline. Their ranks thinned but not stopped, the Marines kept coming, ignoring the exploding cannon shells and small arms fire, at least until a man could ignore them no longer, and fell wounded or dying or dead, and other men stepped over and around him.

Another pair of Hellcats zoomed in on a bunker built around a 105mm cannon, one plane strafing the trenchline, as if to distract the enemy, with the other plane dropping a two-hundred-fifty-pound bomb . . . and then another . . . neither quite hitting the mark, though managing to obliterate the soldiers just outside the bunker. The cannon itself, however, remained unscathed.

And, on the field below, on the move up and over a rocky hillock down under this particular Japanese fortification, the men of the second squad of Second Recon advanced. Maneuvering down the hillside, Sergeant Joe Enders—with Private Ben Yahzee just behind him—jogged along,

Harrigan and Nells at his either side; they formed half of the line of advance, with Hjelmstad, Pappas and Rogers making up the other.

These men had dashed across those bloody beaches yesterday, an obstacle course of the dead, dying and wounded, and because they were valuable—the men of Second Recon—they had been spared the high mortality rate of those first waves ashore. All had made it this far . . . alive, and in one piece—Anderson and Whitehorse included (at least the last time Yahzee had seen them), attached to the first squad.

But now Second Recon had their asses on the front line.

They had just reached the bottom of a small ridge when all hell broke loose—Japs on the ridge above heading down in attack mode, small deadly men in those brown wrapping-paper-colored uniforms, some in netted helmets, others in kepis with neck-protective swatches, some with rifles, others with machine guns, all with seasoned, suntanned faces hard with warfare.

Ben Yahzee was no coward, and he had seen his share of danger in Arizona, from hissing rattlers to bucking broncos, from sandstorms to stampedes. But nothing in his experience—no training lectures, no combat simulations—had prepared him for such carnage. The sky seemed to rain death.

Next to him, Enders was blasting away at the oncoming Japs, the Thompson seemingly having a mind of its own.

"Get your ass behind me!" Enders yelled to him, scowling.

Then the sergeant whirled and Yahzee watched, stunned, as a circle of grassy earth lifted, like a lid, and a Japanese soldier with a rifle in his hands, down in the spider hole, was aiming up at Enders.

But Enders didn't seem to need to aim—his Tommy gun was an extension of him, and he stitched the Jap's chest with bullets that created puffs of dust and blood, killing the man before he could fire even once.

Yahzee thought his perceptions were finely honed—he was a goddamn Indian, after all—but he had no idea how Enders had heard the movement that signaled that spider-holed sniper . . . or had the sergeant caught it in his peripheral vision? Unless in combat, you developed a sixth sense that Yahzee did not yet possess. . . .

Rifle in his hand, heavy radio gear in a pack on his back, Yahzee had yet to get off a round—he was like a visitor here, being escorted across a field of slaughter. In glimpses so quick they barely registered, Yahzee saw other minidramas of combat flash by.

He saw Nells—the original nervous Nellie, probably preoccupied by the bride he'd left at home—playing a game of avoidance, spying a muzzle flash from a spider hole, ducking clear, as the bullets ripped right by him and nailed another Marine bringing up the rear. . . .

And then he saw Harrigan—that blond-haired Florida beach boy, with the Buck Rogers canister backpack that allowed him to throw flames in focused conflagration—step toward that same spider hole and shoot tongues of fire down into it, roasting the enemy alive. Yahzee could see in the wide eyes of Harrigan—a basically gentle soul—that he was as consumed by the horror of what he was doing as the scorched, shrieking soldier was by flames.

Taking cover wherever he could, smart soldier that he was, craggy Gunnery Sergeant Hjelmstad was working the surrounding bushes, firing his twelve-gauge pump-action shotgun as fast as the shells could cycle. Jap soldiers would emerge from the bushes and Hjelmstad would send them screaming back into them, bloody ragdolls. Yahzee had never imagined killing could be such a workman-like procedure.

Chick Rogers—wielding a Browning Automatic Rifle, a big but relatively light automatic weapon— seemed to be having fun! Yahzee had suspected the Texan was crazy, and this confirmed it— Chick's BAR cutting a swath of death across the line of Japs advancing down from the ridge top. Loading up a fresh clip, Chick fumbled a bit as a wounded Jap rose up to settle the score, but the Texan beat him to the punch, two shots dropping the man right at Chick's feet.

The Texan spit tobacco on the corpse, let out his idea of an Indian war whoop—which sickened Yahzee—and pressed on.

Nick Pappas was breathing hard, but nonetheless swung around and, with his M-1, picked off one of two Japs trying to get behind the squad, a head shot, but hit the other one in the body and the guy kept coming, and was right on top of Pappas, who raised his rifle and thrust it forward, the bayonet impaling the soldier.

Pappas withdrew the blade, the Jap fell in a pile before him, and the Greek smiled—not that war-crazy way Chick was displaying, more as if he was surprised by his own resourcefulness, and pleased to still be alive.

Most of these men—like Yahzee—were first-timers in battle, and like him, they were getting a fast lesson in the difference between training and reality.

"Stay on my ass!" Enders yelled again, blasting away.

And Yahzee did as he was told, stunned by the screaming, close quarters, hand-to-hand combat, men fighting and dying all around him, a violent tableau framed by explosions and plumes of choking smoke.

On the run, with that heavy radio pack on his back, Yahzee had trouble getting a decent aim at the adversaries, but—tagging after Enders—few nearby targets remained, anyway. The man was a killing machine, nailing the Japs into their coffins with short, measured bursts of the Thompson.

If Yahzee thought his perceptions of the battleground were surreal, he'd have been shocked to know how utterly Daliesque Enders's own impressions were. Because of his damaged ear, Enders mixed crystal sharp hearing on the one side, with the thunder of war all too clear, the heavy fire of enemy cannons, tanks and mortars, while on his left a dulled, warbling, haunting cacophony throbbed, distant, as if the war were a movie playing in the theater next door.

This created a slowing of time in his perceptions that sent shells tumbling, arcing away from his smoking Tommy gun. It was in this dreamlike state that Enders was able to dispassionately dispatch the enemy to whatever waited beyond this life.

As instructed, Yahzee ran behind Enders, doing his best to keep up, as the squad fought the last few remaining Japs, the ground littered with dead foe and the occasional Marine, none of the squad, thank God, and a bullet whanged alongside Yahzee's helmet, knocking it off.

Enders, seeing this, reached back for the Indian and grabbed him by the arm and, as if he weighed almost nothing, tossed Yahzee into a nearby shell crater. Then Enders flung himself in that same hole, firing as he went, on surrounding bushes, from which a dead Jap tumbled.

Swallowing, Yahzee—small arms fire stopped around them, at least momentarily—reached up and out of their hole and groped for his helmet. He pulled in the tin hat—grooved by the bullet—a moment before bullets from a machine gun ripped across the lip of the crater.

Yahzee lurched back against the far side of the crater, sitting there, as stunned as if he'd been hit with a board, the helmet in his lap. He gazed down at the photo enmeshed in the webbing, and his wife and son—smiling self-consciously for the photographer—looked back at him.

More small arms fire—close by—jarred Yahzee from his momentary reverie, and a Marine dove into the crater, like a kid off the side of a swimming pool . . . only this poor bastard was swimming in his own blood, a stain spreading on his chest while he gasped for breath.

Enders glared at Yahzee. "You gonna piss in that?" he snarled, meaning the helmet, then glanced at the wounded Marine. "Medic!. . . . Put the fucking thing on your head, Private. . . . *Medic!*"

An unfamiliar engine rumble and the crunch of wheels crushing bushes and brush prompted Enders to peek up over the crater rim.

"Fucking great," Enders said, reloading the Thompson.

Yahzee took a peek, and recognized—from Camp Pendleton classwork, not experience—the tank crashing through a thicket as a Ha-Go, Japan's most common tank. Camouflaged, with the Rising Sun flag painted on either side of its rounded turret, the seven-ton Ha-Go had a three-man crew—driver, mechanic/hull gunner and commander, who worked the 37mm main cannon. That weapon and both of the tank's machine guns were chattering away at Marines in their path.

One Marine caught machine-gun fire, and fell, and another Marine stopped and turned, to try to help his buddy, only to catch some of what the other guy got. Then both of them were crushed under tracks containing four wheels in two pairs on either side. The brittle sound of bones breaking provided percussive effects to the Ha-Go's distinctive rumble.

Enders knew the Ha-Go had notoriously poor armor—a mere 12mm thickness—and he blazed away at the beast with his Thompson. He was ducking back down to reload as a medical corpsman, a hard-eyed combat veteran, dove in beside Yahzee and ripped open the shirt of the wounded Marine next to him.

"Put a hand on this!" the corpsman told the Indian.

Yahzee wasn't sure what the medic wanted, exactly, and he extended his hand tentatively; then the corpsman pushed Yahzee's hand down hard on the bloody hole. In moments, the corpsman was pressing a field dressing to the wound, relieving the Navajo of his grisly detail.

That Ha-Go was cresting the ridge now, the very landscape the second squad had fought so hard to own, and Marine positions received deadly strafing from the twin machine guns, sending men scurrying for cover. Some made it.

The clank and roar of another tank, behind them, gave Yahzee a start, but Enders—glancing back that way—shook his head. "It's the cavalry," he said, with no apparent irony.

Yahzee looked back and saw over sixteen tons of armor, firepower and mobility making its way up the incline: an M5A1 Stuart tank, doing 35 mph easy. With its crew of four—driver, bow gunner, main gunner and tank commander—and its 37mm main cannon, pair of .30 caliber machine guns and .50 caliber anti-aircraft machine gun, the Stuart was a better match for the Ha-Go than Enders's Thompson.

The Stuart's cannon boomed and the Ha-Go— struck in the side, just under the Rising Sun flag— blew its hatches, geysering flame.

"Move out!" Hjelmstad called.

And Enders crawled out of the crater, with Yahzee on his tail, the corpsman left behind, still tending that wounded Marine. They and the rest of the second squad rushed forward, seeking better cover, but barely had their run begun when a salvo of artillery fire showered down before them, jerking a coconut tree out by its roots and slamming the thing in front of them, like a roadblock.

The squad dove for cover, as—all around them—war did its frenzied dance to the tune of pounding artillery, hammering machine guns, and clanking tank treads. Below them the Stuart tank positioned itself and began firing on the Japanese lines.

In and around the cannon fire, Gunnery Sergeant Hjelmstad—crouched in a shell hole near a row of bushes with his men—took stock.

Breathing hard, Hjelmstad asked, "Everybody okay?"

Chick Rogers cockily discharged a spent clip from his big BAR. "Still on the hunt, Gunny."

To Yahzee, this was more like being on the wrong end of a target range than any hunt he'd ever been on.

Harrigan said, with a flippancy that didn't quite mask his fear, "They ain't getting rid of me that damn easy."

Next to the beach boy, Nellie called, "Alive and well, Gunny—right, Pappy?"

But Pappas was breathing hard into a paper bag, and didn't seem to hear the question, whether over the cannonfire or his own heaving efforts, that was hard to say.

"What's with the Greek?" Chick asked.

"Prone to hyperventilate," Nellie said.

"Hyper what?" Hjelmstad asked.

Pappas said, "Can't . . . can't breathe . . . breathe good . . . if I get . . . overex . . . excited."

"Bet your sweetie loves that," Chick said with a grin.

Enders gave the Texan a blank stare that conveyed contempt better than any remark.

From where they were, the squad couldn't see the big 105mm cannon in the bunker above them as its barrel swung into a new position. But they felt the repercussion when the shell exploded near the Stuart tank, close enough to knock the Stuart out of commission.

The Stuart's hatches seemed to throw themselves open, and coughing Marines made their hasty exit; but small arms fire from the ridge above cut them down, and the tank commander—about to exit himself—decided instead to stay with his ship. He cranked up the .30 caliber machine gun and blasted away until his belt was empty; as he reloaded, he got cut to pieces by enemy fire.

Cursing in Norwegian, Hjelmstad turned to Yahzee. "Get the Navy on the goddamn horn! Those Japs dug in up there, let's get 'em dug the hell out . . . Enders!"

Enders, scrambling forward, was already peering over the rise, eyeing the big guns. "Target reference dog one," he said, "right seven hundred. Elevation one five zero."

Yahzee, hand-held radio cranked and ready to relay the info, froze—not ten feet in front of him, a Marine got his head blown off . . . not figuratively speaking . . . *blown off*, spurting blood like a red oil well.

"Goddamnit, Yahzee," Enders yelled, furious at the delay, "relay the fucking coordinates!"

Yahzee swallowed, shook the ugly image out of his mind, and spoke into the phonelike receiver, with a shake in his voice that only he noticed.

"*Wol-la-chee gah tkin besh-do-tliz a-kha tsah be-la-sana*," Yahzee said, saying "Arizona" in Navajo code talk. He repeated this, then, using the code, said, "Request fire mission. . . ."

To Enders and the others, this sounded like insane gibberish; but, more important, that was also how it sounded to a Japanese radio team under a camouflaged canopy in an adjacent valley, flipping frantically through American codebooks, with no success.

What Yahzee wanted to hear, however, was a reply from Charlie Whitehorse, who—with his bodyguard Pete "Ox" Anderson—was in the path of those exploding 105 shells.

8

NOT LONG AGO, PETE ANDERSON AND CHARLIE WHITE-
horse and the rest of the first squad had been in
the thick of tanks and advancing troops, a good
half mile behind the second squad, moving across
open ground snarled with crackling brush and
dead grass and trampled weeds.

Then the Japanese cannons, tanks and mortars,
up on the trenchline, had pummeled the battlefield with a series of explosions that created a wall
of fiery death, sending Marines diving for cover,
some making it, others not.

Anderson and Whitehorse found themselves in
a small crater, with rubble from previous explosions providing some shelter even as nearby ex-

plosions continued to rain new debris down on them.

Before long, Whitehorse had received Yahzee's message, and was relaying it in Navajo code to the battleships offshore, requesting support fire on his field radio (which was somewhat bigger than Ben's) while 105 shells slammed to ground all around them, rocking the world.

"*Chuo tkin gah dzeh*," Whitehorse was saying, his voice calm, reflecting the strangely dreamlike state he found himself in, speaking his native tongue in this tropical hell, surrounded by flames and smoke and corpses. "*Ah-losz ah-jah . . .*"

Not ten feet away, one of those corpses rose up, not quite a corpse yet after all, merely a wounded Jap with a blossom of red on his left shoulder and a pistol in his right hand, a pistol aimed right at Whitehorse, who froze in mid-sentence.

Slugs ripped across the Jap's chest, creating more blossoming red and the man's eyes rolled in death and he fell face down on the scraggly earth.

Whitehorse turned toward Anderson, Tommy gun in his hands, smoke curling from its barrel; letting out a breath, the Dineeh warrior nodded his thanks.

Anderson nodded back.

Whitehorse—who had told his friend Ben of his doubts about these Anglo escorts of theirs ("Cowboys don't back up Indians")—suddenly liked the idea of having a bodyguard. He returned to his du-

ties, beginning again with the coded message, requesting Naval guns to squelch those 105
cannons. . . .

Within a minute, half a mile forward, more or
less, Joe Enders saw the first of the Navy's shells
ripping into the earth, landing perhaps fifty yards
behind that bunkered cannon on the ridge.

"Drop fifty," Enders said to Yahzee, still manning
his radio, waiting for the sergeant's instructions.
"Fire for effect."

"*Chindi gah tlo-chin cla-gi-aih,*" Yahzee said into
the receiver, keeping his voice calm despite the
dead and dying all around, "*fir yeh-hes ma-e d-ah
tsah-ah-dzoh.*"

When Yahzee had finished his transmission,
Gunnery Sergeant Hjelmstad, his twelve-gauge at
the ready, yelled, "Move out!"

And the second squad clambered out of the
shell hole and, following their gunnery sergeant,
rushed down the ridge line. As if it had materialized, a clanking, lumbering but oh so beautiful
Stuart tank, equipped for flame-throwing, moved
into their path, and they ducked behind it.

The offshore battleships were responding to
Yahzee's request, letting go with a salvo from their
five-inch cannons. As the squad trailed after the
Stuart tank, the scope of the battlefield vista
amazed Yahzee—the Navy's shells were bracket-
ing the Japanese bunker and its massive 105 cannon, plumes of dark smoke bookending the

concrete, mostly underground structure. Then a direct hit—and an explosion of volcanic magnitude obliterated the bunker, leaving billowing black smoke, leaping flames and a twisted, ravaged cannon barrel.

Up the adjacent hill were trenchlines of Japanese, from which small arms fire emanated; the second squad—like the rest of Second Recon, whose chief job was observation after all—left the mop-up work to the Stuart tank and the platoon of Marines on the vehicle's wheels. As Hjelmstad and Enders and the rest angled down the hill, taking cover in bushes below, the Stuart and those Marines charged up.

The Stuart tank stilled the small arms fire quickly enough, shooting a sixty-foot column of flame into the trenchline, sending Japanese soldiers running for their lives, many of them aflame. A machine gun bunker's palm-log structure fell under the tracks and grinding wheels of the Stuart, which moved back and forth over the logs, like a sadistic child squashing a bug under its heel, soldiers within screaming, others fleeing only to be shot down. Rotating its turret, the Stuart caught the last of the defenders with its machine gun, which for those who'd become human torches was an act of compassion.

Glad not to be part of this, Yahzee suppressed a shudder as he heard screams of agony, followed by the scent of scorched human flesh drifting obscenely on the air.

Soon the Stuart tank had rumbled along on its way, and that platoon of Marines with it, leaving the Second Recon in the bushes, and a Japanese trenchline up the hill that smoldered with shell craters and burning vehicles, littered with dead Japs. A squat metal pill box overlooking the trenches—which the Stuart had not taken time to crush under its powerful wheels—sat silent, no sign of life either from it or the trenches.

Which was what the scouts of Second Recon saw, when they moved up the hill to check those trenchlines for survivors or stragglers; seeing none, they signaled the troops below, and from the bushes emerged the rest of Second Recon (with the exception of the first squad). They were moving forward fairly cautiously, when the pill box came to sudden life, cutting down those scouts in front, sending the rest of the troops scrambling and diving.

Japanese soldiers were springing from hiding places in the trenchline, tiny caves carved out of the earth, and were opening up on the Marines.

"Cover fire!" Hjelmstad yelled to the BAR-wielding Texan, and to the rest of the men, "Rush the line!"

Which they did, screaming their rage and surprise, firing relentlessly, charging the Japanese line with a suicidal frenzy the enemy might have appreciated, had they not been on the receiving end. A few Marines died, but the defenders of the trenches were quickly overwhelmed by the sheer number of the Americans.

Enders leapt into the trench, blazing down the line with his Tommy gun, knocking over Japanese like living bowling pins that were soon dying. He kept blasting, running down the trenchline, side-stepping and leaping over corpses—some fresh and of his own creation, others charred things the Stuart flame-throwing tank had left behind.

Yahzee jumped in behind his bodyguard, and Pappas followed. The Indian got off a few shots, to no particular success, but—as before—Enders was mowing down the enemy before Yahzee could contribute. Pappas was doing well, too, falling in next to the machine-gun-blasting Enders and squeezing off rounds with his M-1 unerringly, the two Marines keeping the path clear, as if Yahzee were a visiting dignitary.

At a wide opening where trenches met, their gunnery sergeant and the rest of second squad—Chick, Harrigan and Nellie—caught up with them. A brief bad moment—during which the two groups almost fired at each other—was followed by nervous grins, and just as a Marine down a ways was standing tall to fire his M-1 at something or other . . .

. . . Enders seemed to sense something (*Is the*

man psychic?, Yahzee wondered) and dove for the rifleman, knocking him into a sandbagged hole within the trench, a moment before machine-gun fire raked where the guy had been standing. Two other Marines, moving along up top, on the edge of the trench, weren't so lucky.

"Guess we know what we gotta do," Enders said, looking back at Harrigan, that walking bomb with the flame-thrower canisters on his back.

Harrigan swallowed, nodded glumly, preparing himself and his equipment.

"I'll cover you," Enders said.

Harrigan, wiping sweat from his eyes, nodded again.

Yahzee glanced at Hjelmstad, who was theoretically in charge; the Norwegian seemed content to defer to Enders, whose battlefield prowess they had all witnessed.

Enders positioned himself and began slinging lead up the slope toward the metal pill box, its central slit like a wide eye staring back at them. Yahzee, staying low, ears filled with Tommy gun chatter, stayed low in the trench, as Harrigan leapt out and dashed toward a crater halfway between them and the pill box.

With Harrigan ducked down there, Enders kept blazing, but machine-gun fire from behind him— a new country heard from!—sent Enders ducking and scrambling down the trench. Yahzee followed him, risking a peek at the source of the new fire: a camouflaged machine gun nest, perhaps twenty feet away.

As Enders moved down the trench, seeking a decent and safer firing position, a Jap scurried out of a hiding place just ahead of them, and Enders stitched him up the back with bullets and sent him sprawling, dead in the dirt.

The recession where the Jap had been hiding, however, provided Enders with a good firing position, and he again let the pill box have the full attention of his Tommy gun. Yahzee, just tagging along, was reeling with the violent fits and starts of combat. . . .

Harrigan, in the meantime, was running toward another, closer-to-the-pill-box crater, into which he and his clumsy flamethrowing gear dove. Enders, seeing this, sought a new position in the trenches, Yahzee at his heels. The Indian almost got clobbered when Enders reared back and hurled a grenade.

The grenade landed and exploded into the expected fragments just in front of the bunker, raising a small dust cloud and, no doubt, stunning the gunners within.

"Bet that got their attention," Enders said.

If it hadn't, what Harrigan did surely would: the battlefront beach boy stood in his crater and unleashed a stream of fire, a terrible orange tongue that licked the metal pill box, sought the slit, slithered inside.

"Yeah," Enders was saying. "Yeah!"

The top of the pill box blew off, then the door.

Through the latter, a pair of screaming Japanese soldiers exited, in flames from head to foot.

Enders ran down the trench, paralleling their fiery departure, and blasted the Japanese, whose screams mercifully ended as they fell in individual flame-crackling piles.

Enders crouched to re-load.

Yahzee was already crouching, trying to escape from the grotesqueries above, only to find himself facing a lifeless carcass, a burned-to-a-crisp corpse with a death mask grin and charred arms reaching out for him; he turned away and another scorched dead man grinned at him from the other side. Wherever he turned, Yahzee found himself mired in horror. . . .

Enders stood, just in time to blast away a Jap leaping into the trench, blowing him back, keeping him out. Running down the trench, Enders stopped—sensing no one on his heels—and glanced back and saw Yahzee, crouched, frozen, looking from grinning charred corpse face to grinning charred corpse face. Had the son of a bitch gone Asiatic already?

"Goddamnit, Yahzee!" he yelled over the drone of battle.

And Yahzee shook his head, swallowed, and yanked himself from the stare of the dead.

Enders—with Yahzee right behind him—

moved quickly back down to where the rest of the Second Recon were returning fire to that machine-gun nest that had almost picked Enders off, earlier.

"I think they got two guns in there, Gunny," Enders said to Hjelmstad.

"We gotta take 'em out." The gunnery sergeant peeked up over the edge of the trench, studying the camouflaged machine gun nest. "Satchel charge!"

A pair of Marines scrambled down the trenches, answering the call, satchels of explosives already in hand.

To the squad, Hjelmstad said, "Rest of you, stay on the line to cover 'em."

Nods all around, as Hjelmstad raised a hand to the two Marines, who had moved into position, ready to run with those charges.

"Fire!" Hjelmstad hollered.

And Enders and the others, Yahzee too, rose up and fired over the lip of the trench, covering for the TNT-toting Marines who were leaping up and out and ducking and dodging their way up the hillside.

But the first of the pair, out in the lead, got cut to shreds by machine-gun fire, barely making it halfway there before he fell, the satchel in dead hands.

The other guy was doing better, making like a running back, weaving, a moving target confounding those machine-gunners, aided by the cover Second Recon was providing . . .

Marines this godforsaken hilly, scrubby stretch of landscape, but he had disobeyed orders doing so.

Finally, the gunnery sergeant said to Yahzee, "Call it in, Private."

"I'll find high ground."

"Do it."

And from the high ground over the battlefield littered with corpses and scorched terrain and cement rubble and gnarled steel, the Dineeh codetalker mumbled into his radio: *"Dah-nes-tsa a-kha shush klesh dzeh moasi ute dah-nes-tsa ah-ah."*

Which meant: "Regimental Objective Baker secure."

From his perch, Yahzee could see movement through the corpses, as Second Recon's first squad trudged up the slope. He noted that Anderson seemed to be ignoring the dead all around them; but Whitehorse—not surprisingly—could not keep his eyes off the bodies. Yahzee understood this: the dead had special significance to the Dineeh . . . dark significance.

Yahzee could also see Enders, over by the remains of the machine-gun nest, sitting on the boulder he'd hidden behind, that had kept him from being ripped apart by shrapnel. His bodyguard seemed to be doing something, but Yahzee couldn't make it out, though he could see Gunnery Sergeant Hjelmstad approaching Enders.

The Indian couldn't hear their conversation, but had he guessed, he'd have been close.

"Another stunt like that shit, Enders," Hjelmstad was saying, "and I'll bust your ass down to private."

Enders said nothing; he was rolling cigarettes, stocking up.

"Of course," Gunny said softly, "you'll probably wind up getting a Congressional Medal for that stupidity, so . . . let's just say, nicely done . . . leave it at that."

Enders remained mute, stayed with his work, and Hjelmstad strode off, apparently sensing Enders's desire to be alone.

Up on the high ground, Whitehorse had joined Yahzee. The two Indians exchanged quiet glances that each was glad the other was still alive.

"Too many dead men," Whitehorse said.

"It's war, Charlie." But the casualness of his reply did not lessen how shaken Yahzee himself felt over what he'd been through, what he'd witnessed. He wondered what his bodyguard was thinking, feeling. . . . Enders could *feel*, couldn't he? Something other than rage?

The codetalker had no way of knowing that Enders—making his homerolleds, stowing them away in the tarnished metal case—was studying a photo tucked in its lid . . . a snapshot of four Marine buddies, three of them dead now.

The only one surviving snapped the lid on the case, fired up a homerolled, and ignored the intrusive gaze of the Indian on the hill.

9

A BLOOD-RED MOON CAST AN EERIE GLOW ACROSS THE
craggy, hard-won landscape, the guns of a newly
installed mortar emplacement blessedly silent after a long day of butchery on both sides. In the
tropical jungle near the brambly battlefield, in a
small clearing with the moonlight filtering through
a thicket that rose well into the sky, in the con-
torted shadows of the outstretched arms of trees,
two Dineeh warriors carried out a ceremony.

Whitehorse had been first: now it was Yahzee's
turn. Yahzee knelt before a small, glowing fire. In
their native language—not a military code—
Whitehorse sang in the haunting, halting chantlike
manner of their people.

The two codetalkers—though Whitehorse had been raised traditionally, and Yahzee modern—had seen more death over these last two days than in their combined lifetimes. And though Yahzee did not share his friend's deep beliefs—that mythical, mystical Dineeh culture centering on the Web of Life—he had nonetheless absorbed his people's uneasy attitude toward death.

To the Dineeh, death released evil spirits; many a hogan had been burned after someone had died within—many an elderly Indian had wandered off into the desert to die alone, and spare his loved ones the dangerous presence of evil spirits that dying unleashed.

Certain ceremonies could battle these evil spirits—and Yahzee, having aided Whitehorse in undergoing the Evil Way ritual, was now having that ceremony performed on him. Rubbing his hands on charred firewood, Whitehorse turned to the kneeling, stone-faced Yahzee and smeared ash on his friend's cheeks.

Then Whitehorse removed from around his neck, where it had been dangling on a leather cord, a deerskin pouch, from which he poured some of its contents into his palm: corn pollen. Some of this he dabbed onto Yahzee's forehead, sprinkling more on the scraggy earth around him.

After staring silently at the ground for several long moments, Whitehorse looked at his friend, who was gazing straight ahead, into nothing, or perhaps into everything; and Whitehorse again began to chant, whispering now.

"I see you a warrior, Yahzee," Whitehorse said in the tongue of the Dineeh, "and you will make our people proud."

Elsewhere, along the edge of the battlefield where the Marines of Second Recon had bivouacked, men were pitching their shelter halfs, preparing to sleep under their rain-protective ponchos.

Nells tilted his wristwatch to catch the moonlight, and sent a question in the general direction of Harrigan and Pappas, who were settling in for the night.

"Twenty-two hundred hours here in hell," Nells said. "What's that make it back on the East Coast?"

Pappas farted with his lips. "Do I look like fuckin' Greenwich mean time?"

Nells, still studying his watch, calculating, said, "It's seven—no, eight A.M. Sunday morning."

"Time for church," Harrigan said.

But Nells looked glum. "I just hope my side of the bed didn't get filled up, Saturday night."

Pappas shook his head. "You're gonna save the Japs the trouble, if you don't cut it out, Nellie."

"Huh?"

"You'll kill yourself worrying about that skirt. You want to give yourself a goddamn ulcer?"

"Yeah . . . yeah." Nells sighed and crawled into

his little tent, head hanging out the front to keep conversation going. "You're probably right. . . . Hey, you think if I gave myself an ulcer they'd send me home?"

"Rhode Island don't have the market cornered on dames," Harrigan said, on his back, elbows winged, staring up at the red moon, an unlighted cigarette dangling. "Plenty of babes in this old world. . . ."

"Not for me," Nells said. "Not for me."

"Well," Pappas said, sitting like an Indian in front of his tent, "there sure as hell ain't any dolls around this godforsaken cow pasture. . . . You gonna light that smoke, Harry?"

Harrigan, who had spent the day operating a flamethrower, after all, seemed to flinch at that remark. "What do you mean?"

"I mean, you can light the goddamned thing without us all exploding. You keep an unlit fag in your mouth like that, people might start to talk. . . ."

"Ah, fuck you, Pappy." Eyes on the sky again, the unlit cigarette bobbling, Harrigan said, "You want to see beautiful women? Try where I come from. . . . Daytona Beach, nothing like it. Six months ago I was lyin' on the sand and this sweet little piece comes drippin' out of the water in a bathing suit that didn't leave a thing to the imagination. Comes right up to me and says her name is Mollie . . . and do I know where the weenie roast is?"

Pappas laughed at that; so did Nells, a little.

"Now I'm stuck on this hellhole," Harrigan said, "a roman candle on my back. . . . roasting more than goddamn weenies. . . . Why the hell I volunteered, is way the fuck beyond me."

"Never volunteer," Pappas said, reiterating the code of all Marines.

The Texan, Chick, walked up, joining them, having already pitched his shelter half.

"Better than getting drafted," he reminded them. He sat in front of his little tent. "Get drafted, you wind up in the damn Army. With all the riffraff that didn't wanna go. Hell, if I'm going to fight, I'm gonna fight alongside the best."

"Semper fi, Mac," Pappas said, nodding.

Chick continued: "My old man was a Marine. He was an asskicker on land and sea . . . one hell of an asskicker. Hell of a Marine."

Nells had apparently not been paying much attention to any of this, his mind still in Rhode Island with his bride. He turned to Pappas, in the tent next to him, and said softly, "Do me a favor, Pap—should something happen to. . . . Well, why don't you go ahead and keep this for me?"

Pappas looked alarmed at the sight of Nells holding out his wedding ring.

The handsome boy's mouth was quivering. "See

that this gets back to Betty. . . . She picked it out
and all."

"Put that goddamn thing back on," Pappas said.
"Don't talk that way. You decide you're gonna buy
it, Christ, you can bank on it. Quit that thinking!"

Nells mumbled, "Okay," and slipped the ring
back on.

"Don't even kid about it. Jesus."

But everybody knew Nells had not been kidding.
Everybody had seen the fresh graves not so far
from where they slept—other soldiers sleeping
with their resting spot marked by rifles jammed
bayonet-first into the dirt, empty helmets propped
on top.

At the moment, Pete Anderson—a tin cup of
coffee in either hand—was whistling past that impromptu graveyard, and heading up a slope to
where he'd noticed Joe Enders had gone off, typically, to be alone. Despite this, Anderson craved
Enders's company, because his fellow bodyguard
alone among these men shared the terrible secret
of their true orders.

Enders sat on a rise staring down the far side at
the opening in the trees where the embers of a dying fire flickered and two Indians carried out their
own secret ceremonies, Whitehorse's chanting
drifting strangely on the wind as if even now these
two were sending out code into the night.

Though Anderson was coming up on his left

side, Enders sensed him, and glanced up as Anderson held out a cup of coffee.

"Good for what ails you," Anderson said.

Enders took the steaming cup, nodded his thanks.

Anderson got down on his haunches, gestured toward the Indians below. "What the hell are they doing?"

"I don't know, but they've been at it since sundown."

Anderson sipped his coffee. "Kinda sounds like they're praying."

"Maybe so, but it's not for forgiveness. At least not Yahzee."

"What do you mean?"

"That Indian warrior of mine didn't shoot so much as a squirrel today."

Anderson sipped some more coffee, smirked a bit. "You and your Tommy gun don't leave much for anybody else to do. That was some John Wayne routine you pulled, rushing that machine-gun nest."

Enders grunted. Drank some coffee.

The chanting echoed softly up to them.

"Could be they're praying 'cause they know our orders," Anderson said.

"Skip it."

Anderson shrugged, set his cup down on the ground. He withdrew a letter from his pocket, sniffed its sweet perfume-soaked paper. The light of the moon revealed the return address—the WAVE Barracks at Paradise Cove, Hawaii.

"I dream of going back to Paradise Cove every night," Anderson said.

"Tonight you may dream of something else."

"Combat, you mean?"

"You'll see."

"Goddamn, but you're pleasant company. Here. This letter is yours."

Enders glanced at Anderson, surprised. But he took the letter that Anderson had brought him.

"It's from that girl Rita, right? Nice. A real beauty."

Enders put the letter down on a rock next to him. "That's something else we won't be talking about."

"You're a joy to know, Enders."

The Navajo chanting kept drifting up to them, otherworldly, bizarrely beautiful.

"Joe?"

"What?"

"Do you . . . do you think you could do it?"

"Do what?"

"You know what I'm talking about."

"We're not discussing that, either."

"What if I need to 'discuss' it?"

"Give it a rest, Anderson."

"Oh, believe me, I try, I try. . . . But how can they expect a man to—"

"We're not men," Enders said, lighting up a homerolled, "we're Marines."

But Anderson could tell, for all Enders's coldness, he too was affected—otherwise why would he be staring down at those Navajos, as lost in their chanting as they were?

What Anderson could not know was that even as Enders's good ear reported the Navajo ceremony to him, lucid in the stillness of the night, his other ear, the damaged one, locked in his head other sounds, sounds that replayed in his mind, in his dreams—he'd told Anderson such dreams awaited—explosions, screams, the screams of dying Marines, warped, surreal, but very much there, one voice, the voice of a man dead for many months now, Mertens, chanting his own obscene prayer: *goddamn you, Enders! Goddamn you, Enders!*

Enders jerked upright, awake—it was hours later now, and his hard-breathing, sweating body was a rigid exclamation point in the slumbering sentence of the Marines of the Second Recon around him. Sleeping under his poncho in a hole he'd dug himself—no shelter half for him—Enders took air in and out, slowly, calming himself, clearing his mind of combat images, that fever dream melding of Guadalcanal and Saipan.

He felt eyes on him, and quickly turned.

Yahzee was sitting there, in his own hole, poncho

draped over him, as still as a statue, gazing at Enders . . . and the eyes of these two Marines locked.

"It's called an Evil Way ceremony," Yahzee said softly.

". . . What is?"

"What you saw us doing—Charlie and me. The Dineeh . . . the Navajo . . . believe until a body's given proper burial, the spirit stays near it. Many times *chendis*—evil spirits—are released."

"What—ghosts?"

Yahzee looked at the red moon. "My people call that a butcher's moon—blood on its face. Fitting, after today. . . . I haven't thought much about any of this stuff, not since, hell, since I was a kid. Seeing all those dead men today brought it back."

"You seeing ghosts, Private? Rising off the corpses like, what? Steam?"

"I saw no ghosts."

"Good for you."

"I'm telling you this because . . . I want you to know that won't happen again."

"What won't?"

"I won't . . . freeze up again."

"Why? 'Cause your pal smeared ash on your face?"

Yahzee nodded. " 'Cause my pal smeared ash on my face."

Enders snorted, and rolled over, turning his back to the Indian—enough of this latenight bullshit chit-chat. But he could feel Yahzee's eyes on him, still, and when the Navajo spoke, Enders was not surprised.

"Sergeant—I don't think I'm the only one who needs a little medicine."

Enders turned back over, glared at Yahzee; had the Indian seen him taking the pills Rita gave him? Or was Yahzee referring to him waking up in a cold sweat after those nightmares?

"What do you mean by that?" Enders asked, an edge in his voice.

Yahzee paused, seemed about to reply, then—apparently thinking better of it—lay down and pulled the poncho over himself like a blanket.

It took a long time for either man to fall asleep . . . but their conversation, on this night after a terrible day of combat, was over.

The next morning, Yahzee noticed the diamond shimmer of water through the trees and made his way through the undergrowth to a rock-rimmed stream, sparkling in the early sunlight. Leaving his green dungaree shirt on a branch and his boots and helmet below, he waded in till he was knee-deep in the bracing coolness, then reached down and scooped up handful after handful of water and refreshed and washed himself.

When he returned barefoot and barechested, reaching out for his shirt on that branch, a rifle barrel poked out of the thicket, and he froze . . . and for seconds that seemed like minutes he wondered if he had just taken his last bath. . . .

Then a voice from the bushes—an unmistakable Texas drawl—said, "What in the Sam Hill have we got here?"

Yahzee relaxed. Chick was no prize, but at least he wasn't a Jap.

Rogers and Pappas, in full uniform sans helmet, pushed through the bushes and joined Yahzee along the rocky bank of the stream.

Yahzee grinned. "I was just trying to get the damn bugs out of my hair."

Then he reached for his dungaree shirt, and Chick thrust his bayonet between Yahzee and his clothes.

"What are you doin', boy?" Chick asked, something nasty in the drawl now.

"I'm gonna put my uniform on, Chick."

"Your uniform? What would a Jap want with an American uniform? Are you a spy?" Chick grinned sideways at Pappas, who seemed embarrassed by this display of bullying bigotry.

Yahzee didn't bother trying to disguise how irritated he was; let Charlie Whitehorse play the impassive noble red man—Ben Yahzee was pissed.

"You gonna let me get my clothes on, Chick? Or are you having too good a time showing what an ignorant jackass you can be?"

Chick's eyes flared, his cheeks reddened, and

he handed Pappas his rifle and gave the Indian a long, slow look . . . then he lashed out, knocking Yahzee back into the stream, with a splash that got himself and Pappas wet.

Pappas, shaking the moisture off like a dog that just got an unwanted bath, was rolling his eyes, saying, "Fuck a duck, Chick! What the hell d'you do that for?"

Yahzee came up and out of the stream and headed for that branch . . . and Chick again inserted himself between the Indian and his goal. Yahzee shoved Chick out of the way, but the Texan threw a straight-arm into the Navajo that sent him tumbling back into the water—less of a splash this time; no less indignity, though.

Pappas was shaking his head. "Oh, shit. . . ."

Yahzee rose in the shallow water and just stood there, staring stoically at the Texan. Then the Indian, moving with slow determination, strode out of the stream and pushed Chick aside, but when Chick went to lash out again, Yahzee ducked and swung his leg and caught Chick behind the knees, upending him, sending him tumbling, careening, windmilling backward into the water, where he made a hell of a splash.

"Whoops," Pappas said.

Chick charged out like a bull, dripping wet, steaming mad, rushing toward Yahzee, tackling him, bringing him down, climbing on top of him, drawing back a fist . . .

. . . but that fist never delivered its punch to the pinned Indian, as a hand clamped onto it and another hand settled on Chick's shoulder and wrenched him back, hard, off Yahzee.

Enders almost smiled as the Texan howled, and when Chick tried to fight back, to squirm free, Enders twisted that wrist behind the Texan and applied pressure while asking, calmly if through gritted teeth, "You about done, Corporal?"

Chick fought for a few more seconds, then went limp in surrender, and Enders shoved him to the rocky shore. Pappas was over helping Yahzee up, asking him if he was okay.

"Yeah, I'm okay," Yahzee said.

"You sure, Ben?"

Yahzee was surprised to hear himself called by his first name by one of the white Marines. Nodding, he said, "I'm okay, Pappy."

Chick squinted and pretended to be looking close at Ben, for the first time. "What—is that Yahzee? Hell, I thought it was some Nip who killed some poor jarhead for his uniform."

Yahzee laughed once, without humor, at Chick's horseshit effort to cover his ass.

"Maybe you need glasses, Chick," Enders said, coldly.

"Well, hell," the Texan said, gesturing wildly, "he looks like one, don't he? I mean, isn't that what you're doin' here, Enders? Makin' sure these damn Injuns ain't taken for Japs?"

"I am not a 'damn Injun,' " Yahzee said, stepping right up to Chick. "I'm of the Dineeh . . . what some call Navajo. Of the Bitter Water People, born for the Towering House Clan."

And he went to the branch to collect his shirt and get into his boots.

Pappas, disgusted, said to Chick, "He's also an American, you redneck asshole."

"Hey, watch your damn mouth!" Chick said. "Show a little respect."

Then Chick and Pappas disappeared off through the brush, leaving Enders and Yahzee alone.

Yahzee was buttoning his shirt when Enders tossed the Indian his helmet.

"Thank you," Yahzee said.

Enders sneered at him. "Chick's right—you do look like a damn Jap. Next time you wanna go wandering off, I don't care if it's for a bath or a dump, you tell me first—get it? Otherwise, I'll be the one kicking your red ass."

They walked back to camp together, without a word.

10

AS TRUCK WHEELS GROUND THEIR CRUNCHING WAY UP a steep red clay road, leaving behind the mortar encampment won by the bravery and blood of the Second Marines, an envelope—kissed by the wind—drifted across thirty fresh helmet-and-bayonet-markered graves. The envelope—unopened—contained a letter to a certain Sergeant Joe Enders, from one Rita Swelton, WAVE nurse.

In it she spoke of numerous inconsequential things—like the stray dog she'd found on Waikiki beach that had so reminded her of Joe she'd named it after him, a mutt she had given a bath and with whom she was currently sharing her bed. Nothing about the war, not directly, just a warm if oddly tentative how-the-hell-are-you letter that wondered if he would ("given that you're not much of a writer") bother to answer.

The young woman would never have guessed her missive might go unread, much less not generate a reply, as it skipped and tripped on the wind, dancing across graves of Marines, any one of whom would have given their left one for just such comfort from a beautiful girl back home . . . had these men not already given much more than that.

As the convoy of big diesel trucks rolled away, various vehicles heading for assorted vectors, Yahzee—on a bench next to Hjelmstad and Nellie, opposite another bench where Pappas, Chick and Harrigan rumble-rode, with Enders right across from him—watched as a truck bearing the first squad turned off in its own direction. He lifted a hand in a wish of good luck to Whitehorse, who did the same for him, and then was gone.

Enders and Yahzee were each at the respective end of their bench, near the whistle and whip of wind. The morose sergeant sat silently, somehow apart from the rest of them, though sitting right next to Pappas.

Yahzee knew all too well that Enders hadn't slept good last night—that the bodyguard's periodic nightmares had awakened both of them; and right now Enders was hunkered, arms folded, helmet tipped over his eyes, obviously trying to catch up on last night's lost shuteye.

They were one of a small convoy of trucks rolling along a jungle road through a coconut grove, their vehicle bringing up the rear. The road was dirt, of course, a glorified path, badly rutted, and one memorable bump caused Yahzee—working on a letter home, using his pack as a portable desk—to mess up his writing, a perfectly good English word turned into a meaningless scrawl.

The jostle was severe enough to awaken Enders, who peered under his helmet at Yahzee, and said, "What the hell are *you* doing?"

"Writing a letter."

"Writing a letter."

"Yeah, writing a letter—to my son."

"You forget your orders? No letters out."

Yahzee kept writing—he was signing off, sending his love. "I know my orders."

"Yeah? Well, command don't want postmarks going to the reservation."

Yahzee kept writing.

"You hear me, Yahzee?" Enders said, his voice sharp, tone nasty.

Several of the second squad members down either bench were eavesdropping now, exchanging glances, wondering if a confrontation was coming—something that had seemed to all of them to be brewing for days, now.

But Yahzee was folding the letter carefully, placing it into an unaddressed envelope; he slipped it into his pack next to at least a dozen other unsent letters.

Yahzee looked up at Enders without animosity, shrugged, said, "I thought he might read them, later . . . when I get home."

Enders swallowed. He twitched a one-sided non-smile.

For a moment there, Yahzee thought he might have seen embarrassment in those cold eyes. But Enders seemed only to lapse into another brooding silence, and Yahzee almost jumped when the bodyguard suddenly asked a question.

"Your son," Enders said, "what's his name?"

Stunned by Enders's interest, Yahzee said, "George. His name is George."

"Good American name."

"You don't know the half of it—his middle name's Washington . . . George Washington Yahzee."

A tiny smile formed on Enders's grim countenance. "You know, that's got a nice ring to it."

Now it was Yahzee who felt a flush of embarrassment. "Well, my wife wasn't so sure. She's a little more on the . . . traditional side."

"Like your buddy Whitehorse."

"Yeah. Like Charlie." Yahzee took his helmet off and handed it toward Enders, who seemed surprised, until he realized Yahzee was tipping it forward for him to get a look at the family photo tucked in the webbing.

Enders took a brief look and, obviously ill at ease, handed the helmet back. "Nice looking family," he said, noncommittally.

Yahzee sensed something in what seemed a cordial if cool response from Enders—it was as if the sergeant, seeing the wife and three-year-old Yahzee had left behind, were learning more than he needed to know, or wanted to know, about his charge. What was it, Yahzee wondered, that made Enders seem so determined to maintain a distance from him? They were assigned together; sure, he knew that when men became friends in combat, they risked the emotional mutilation of losing somebody close . . . but this seemed different . . . this was something else. . . .

But Yahzee kept trying, seizing on this small opening.

"Yeah, George is a real character," he said conversationally. "Got a mind of his own. Stubborn little mule."

Enders—opening his tarnished metal cigarette case, selecting a homerolled—merely nodded.

"Can I try one of those things?" Yahzee asked.

"I never saw you smoke."

"Lots of guys learn to smoke in combat."

"That's the truth."

"Anyway, I like to stay open to new experiences."

Enders just stared at Yahzee for a while, as if the Indian had asked for a hundred dollars, not a damn cigarette.

Finally, the sergeant—after lighting up his own ciggie—handed one of the homerolleds over to the private, and fired up his Zippo, to give Yahzee a light, but it never happened, and it was as if thumbing the lighter had caused an enormous explosion, rocking not just the truck but Saipan itself.

From their benches the second squad hadn't seen it, but a shell had made a direct hit on the truck just ahead of them, obliterating the vehicle and the men within. Their own truck, its driver alert, swerved around the blast crater, careening wildly off on the dusty shoulder, shaking the men in the back like a box of Chiclets.

Another explosion, again just ahead of them, flipped the truck into the air and spilled the men out onto the rough ground, and suddenly the second squad was diving, scrambling, hoping to keep from getting crushed by the diesel, which hit hard, killing its driver but not, thank God, creating yet another explosion.

Massive blasts continuing, Enders pushed the stunned Yahzee off the road, the Indian burdened by the heavy radio gear on his back, hauling him toward the lower slopes of Mount Tipo Pale, along which they'd been travelling. The shelling, coming hard and heavy, seemed to be targeting the road, and if they got up into the rocks, away from the shelling (Enders felt), they'd have a chance.

Just behind them another shell-invoked explosion shook the earth and Enders saw Yahzee lurch, something slamming him in the back, knocking him down like God had slapped him.

"I'm hit!" the Indian yelled. "It burns!"

Enders latched onto a shoulder strap and yanked Yahzee along, dragging him to cover behind an outcropping of rocks, where the entire second squad . . . no casualties, not yet . . . had scrambled. Shell after shell was hitting the road, turning it into the surface of the moon, rubble and steel flying like scalding hailstones.

Sitting there, his face a mask of pain, Yahzee moaned. "Damn, it burns. . . ."

Behind the relative shelter of the rocks, even as shells sent their thunder again and again, Enders rolled Yahzee over on his belly and yanked the Navajo's dungaree shirt out of his trousers and ripped the heavy cloth, exposing a red-hot sliver of shrapnel sizzling on the Indian's skin at the base of his spine. Enders flicked it off like a bug.

"You ain't hit," he said.

Yahzee was breathing hard, but clearly the pain had already eased. "Huh?"

"Just shrapnel; you're burned but not cut. You'll live . . . Same can't be said for your radio."

The radio pack on his upper back was sparking, shattered by a rain of shrapnel—the bulky thing had no doubt saved the Indian's life. But Enders now was faced with baby-sitting duty for a "kid" who served no fucking combat purpose.

"Where the hell are those shells coming from?" Hjelmstad asked, over on the other side of the huddled Marines.

Chick peeked over the rocks at where the road used to be, at the ever-forming craters, which were huge. "Goddamn," the Texan said. "There wasn't supposed to be no cannon in this sector!"

"There isn't," Enders said.

Everybody looked at him, and Enders nodded back toward the U.S. lines.

Hjelmstad's eyes got huge. "You mean, they're ours?" His accent seemed to thicken in stress, "they're" becoming "dere."

"Those are howitzers," Pappas said, also saucer-eyed. "U.S. howitzers?"

"Bingo," Enders said, and another blast sent rock and ash and steel pluming into the air.

Behind the relative safety of the outcropping, Pappas withdrew a map from his pack and smoothed it out, squinting at the paper—they were all blinking and shielding their eyes in the small duststorm the shells were stirring up.

"We're supposed to be on road O4." Pappas reported.

"Well, we don't seem to be," Hjelmstad said. The gunnery sergeant turned to his codetalker. "Yahzee, get on the horn—tell Regiment they're shellin' the shit out of their own people!"

Yahzee had slung the radio off his back. "Radio's out, Gunny—shrapnel ate it."

Hjelmstad cursed in Norwegian, and, as if in reply, another round of multiple explosions showered down, closer to their position.

"Move!" Hjelmstad said, and the second squad needed no further prodding, following their gunnery sergeant up the slope, hustling out of harm's way.

The ground was rocky, yet much of the terrain retained a jungle aspect, and running from that friendly fire was no picnic. Enders was just starting to feel like they were getting into safe territory when three rounds ripped the area, from a row of trees up ahead.

"Down," Hjelmstad yelled, but everybody had already hit the deck . . .

. . . except for Enders, who had pulled Yahzee out of firing range, having seen the muzzle flashes, and knowing these weren't snipers, but scouts. He could see the sons of bitches, moving through those trees and the vapor-like dust, the pair pausing now before firing again, to signal somebody nearby—just the time Enders needed to cut the bastards down, his Tommy gun taking them in a quick burst, dead before they could scream.

Enders moved forward and so did the rest of the squad, Hjelmstad again deferring to the sergeant, and they heard the machine-gun fire, from further up the hillside, and again hugged the rocks, but not before they had seen through the haze of drifting ash not just muzzle flash but an

Nicolas Cage plays Joe Enders, a Marine in the Pacific Theater of World War II driven to acts of extreme heroism by tormented memories.

Enders spends months in the hospital with a severe head wound; he is the only survivor of his unit.

Frances O'Connor plays Rita, the beautiful and compassionate WAVE who befriends Enders.

The Second Recon—Enders's new unit.

Ben Yahzee (Adam Beach) is the Navajo codetalker whom Enders (Nicolas Cage) is assigned to protect—so that the code never falls into enemy hands.

Ox Anderson (Christian Slater), the other codetalker bodyguard, is the only one who knows and shares Enders's secret mission.

The Second Squad gets their assignment—Saipan.

The Japanese resistance on Saipan is far tougher than military intelligence predicted. Enders, Yahzee, and the Second Squad are in the thick of the fighting.

Yahzee's friend Whitehorse (Roger Willie) helps him purge the spirits of the dead in a solemn Navajo ceremony.

Enders finally tells a sympathetic Yahzee some of the burdens he carries.

The Japanese never broke the Navajo code. It—and the key role played by Navajo soldiers in World War II—remained a military secret until twenty-five years later.

The Second Squadron advances together on the Japanese line amid terrible bloodshed.

entire goddamn platoon less than a hundred yards ahead, manning a trenchline with rifles and machine guns.

Hunkering down in the rocks, a floating fog of shell-stirred dust urging them to cough, the second squad now faced the Jap line on one side and the salvo of "friendly" howitzers on the other.

Pappas said, "This must be that rock-and-a-hard-place you hear so much about."

Enders stood and threw Thompson fire at the Japs, then dropped back down, half a second before machine gun shells smacked the rocks inches above his head, biting off little fragments and spitting them out.

Two more American shells pounded the earth, sending shrapnel ripping through the air, and the second squad hugged the ground. A momentary lull followed, and Yahzee had a closer look at his radio, which he was still lugging with him; his training at Pendleton included repair, but this was a hopeless case, damn thing was shattered to shit. . . .

Another shell erupted, closer, too close, and they scrambled forward for new cover, despite narrowing the distance between them and that Jap trenchline. As they ran, Hjelmstad tripped over one of the dead scouts Enders had nailed, going ass over teakettle; it might have been funny if death weren't so much a part of the equation.

Bunched together in another rocky nook,

Hjelmstad had scurried in next to Yahzee, who was staring at the nearby corpse that the gunnery sergeant had stumbled over.

"You okay, Yahzee?" Hjelmstad asked over Jap machine-gun fire, an absurd question considering the circumstances.

Yahzee said nothing.

Enders fired a blast, then ducked down, ejected a spent clip, slammed in a new one, and glared at Yahzee. "Seeing ghosts again?"

Yahzee wasn't sure he should say what he was thinking; tactics weren't his job, after all. But he bit his lip and said, "You were right, Joe."

"Huh?"

"I do look like a damn Jap."

That stopped Enders. He looked over at the dead soldier and noted the similarity of features to the Navajo's, the high cheekbones, narrow eyes, dark complexion. He knew at once what the codetalker meant, and he shook his head.

"No way, Private."

Hjelmstad was slamming in a fresh clip. "What the hell you girls talkin' about?"

Yahzee nodded to the scout; he spoke with assurance, or tried to, anyway. "I'm talking about putting on that Japanese uniform."

"Why the hell?" the gunnery sergeant asked.

Enders said, "He wants to get ahold of one of their radios."

Yahzee nodded again, said, "And call off our guns, yes."

Enders was still shaking his head, dismayed to see Hjelmstad looking from the dead man back to Yahzee, and from Yahzee to the dead man, wheels turning. . . .

"Gunny," Enders said, and a lull in the firing allowed him to speak softly, "he goes out there, gets killed, we got no codetalker."

"Without a radio we got no codetalker, already," Hjelmstad pointed out.

"What if he gets captured? I can't let that—"

"Who died and put you in charge, Enders?"

An enemy volley ripped in, and Enders and Hjelmstad interrupted their chat to join the rest of the squad in sending a few rounds back.

When they'd ducked down again, Enders said to the gunnery sergeant, "I got orders. The codetalker is *my* responsibility."

"Yeah, and you and him and every man in this outfit is mine!"

Another explosion, way the hell too close, threw rock and ash in the air, like demented, dangerous confetti, a blast of battle heat washing over them.

Nellie and Pappas had been closest to it, and Pappas, in addition to that hot wave of air, felt something slam down next to him. In the aftermath of the explosion, he turned and saw what it was: the lifeless form of John Nells.

"They got Nellie!" Pappas yelled. "Shit, they got Nellie!"

They got him, all right: the handsome boy's blank-eyed face was recognizable, but the rest of him was a bloody pincushion of shrapnel, and his left arm was gone, the stump leaching blood.

"His ring," Pappas mumbled. "Where's his fucking ring? His wife . . . he wanted her . . . where's his fucking wedding ring?"

The Greek stood, his back to the Japanese fire, facing down toward the road, and he screamed, "You sons of bitches, you're killing us! You're killing your own—"

That was when Chick yanked Pappas down, both of them barely missing a burst of enemy rifle fire. The Texan held his friend in big bear hug and Pappas wilted into it, sobbing, sickened, helpless.

"Name was Betty . . . wanted her to have it. . . ."

"Pappy," Chick said, patting the Greek on the back like a baby, "it's okay, it's okay. . . ."

But they all knew it wasn't.

All of them knew they'd been lucky to make it this far without losing one of their own—but this was the first, and the loss hit them hard. Yahzee was staring at the corpse, not the first time he'd reacted with stunned silence to the sight of combat death; but this time, so was Enders.

"Well, that fuckin' tears it," Hjelmstad said. He turned to the Navajo. "Okay, then—let's do it. Strip the Nip."

Yahzee, hardly believing this idea had been his own, swallowed and went over there and, with Hjelmstad's help, undressed the Japanese corpse, yanking off his boots.

Enders helped.

11

HOPING THE SCORCHED, SOMEWHAT BLOODY BULLET HOLES across the garment's belly wouldn't be noticed, Ben Yahzee buttoned his tunic—or rather, the dead Jap soldier's tunic—and nodded to Hjelmstad, indicating he was ready to undertake this mission.

Working his voice up over the din of bullets and bombs, the gunnery sergeant asked, "You sure you're up to this, Private?"

"Only one way to find out," the Indian said, snugging on the Jap cap with kepi with one hand, and with the other handing the Norwegian his helmet. "For safekeeping."

Hjelmstad seemed confused for a moment, then noticed the family photo caught inside the helmet's webbing. He nodded. "They'll be fine right here with me."

Nearby, Enders had pulled his .45 and was chambering a round; he snugged the automatic behind him, at the base of his spine, under his un-tucked dungaree shirt.

Hjelmstad took this in skeptically. "What the hell you think you're doing, Enders?"

"Following my orders," he said, "and sticking with the codetalker."

"You're going with him?"

"If that's okay with you. . . ." He turned to Yahzee. "Repeat after me: *horyo*."

Yahzee and Hjelmstad just looked at him.

"It's Japanese for 'prisoner,' you chowerheads. Let's hear it, Yahzee."

"*Horyo*," the Indian said.

"Poof," Enders said, "you're a Jap."

Punctuating his sentence, another huge shell hit hard, not fifty yards behind them, stirring up billowing, blinding dust. The day was quickly be-coming an otherworldly night.

"Goddamn!" Pappas said, shielding his eyes.

"You mean, thank God," Enders said. He turned to the Navajo codetalker in the Japanese uniform. "We can *use* this. . . . Let's go, Tojo. . . ."

At the Japanese frontline, down in their trenches and in the encampment beyond, soldiers waited at their rifles and machine guns, tense as

clenched fists, their vision impaired, even ob-
scured, by the drifting ash. The barrage of shells
hammering at the heels of those Marines down
there, courtesy of their own big American guns,
might have provided a sense of smug satisfaction
for these troops if they hadn't felt lost themselves
in the sooty dust storm that the pounding shells
continued to spur. Machine gunners, whenever
the swirl of black dust allowed, fired down toward
the Americans, red-orange muzzle flash cutting
through the black cloud like flares. But the war
had suddenly become strangely abstract. . . .

Standing point in a slit trench a few yards forward of the line, a pair of the Rising Sun's finest
squinted into the swirling darkness, one covering
his mouth with a rag, hoping to keep the ash out of
his lungs, the other glancing up through the shell-
stirred tempest now and then at the pale sun, as if
to make sure it were still there.

A voice called out to them, startling them: *"Horyo! Horyo!"*

That one word of their language had been flung
their way was enough only to keep these sentinels
from opening fire: their rifles were tensely at the
ready. Through the billowing, choking ash, two
figures emerged, silhouettes moving toward them,
then materializing as a Nipponese scout and his
American Marine prisoner.

"Horyo!" Ben Yahzee called out, exhausting his
entire Japanese vocabulary.

Enders held his hands high, hanging his head low, a sorry specimen of a beaten foe. Behind him, Yahzee prodded Enders's back shakily, with the confiscated bayoneted rifle, which the Indian held in a manner designed to hide the bullet holes in his tunic's midsection.

"*Horyo!*" Yahzee said, edgy, feeling like he was saying "Hello" to these Japs in a bad imitation of their own pidgin English.

But the point men passed them along, and within seconds, Yahzee was shoving Enders down into a trench, jumping in after, walking his bodyguard down a gauntlet of kicks and shoves and taunts; one whack from a gun butt caused that concealed .45 to pop out of Enders's waistband in back and hit the dirt. Yahzee scooped up the .45, shoved it in his own belt, in front, and thumped Enders on the back for hiding the pistol.

Several Japanese began cursing their scout for not checking better for weapons, but neither Yahzee nor Enders had any idea what all this shouting was about . . . only that it was disturbing as hell to both of them. They just kept moving, captor and prisoner—"*Horyo!*"

When they came up out of the trenchline, into the encampment—the dust having cleared, some—a sergeant approached, eyeing them suspiciously.

"What unit are you?" the sergeant asked in Japanese.

Yahzee just kept moving quickly, as if he hadn't heard the man.

"What unit are you?" the sergeant shouted.

Enders whispered, "Now."

On cue, Yahzee swung the butt of the rifle up and smacked Enders in the upper back, but not as hard as it looked, not really hard enough to knock Enders down . . . though down he went.

And Gunnery Sergeant Hjelmstad, watching through the sooty haze as best he could with field glasses, saw the prearranged signal, and he, too, called, "Now!"

Chick jumped to his feet and let go with the BAR and the rest of second squad poured it on, too, sending heavy fire toward the Jap line.

This was enough to make the Japanese sergeant and his gunners forget all about the scout with the prisoner (and the limited vocabulary), and they dove into the trenches for cover, and to return fire on those damned Americans below.

Keeping down, moving swiftly behind enemy lines, Yahzee and Enders headed toward the high point they had both spotted, figuring this the obvious likely location of the encampment's radio crew. On the way, they almost stepped into another slit trench, occupied by a rifleman, who looked up at them in surprise.

"*Horyo!*" Yahzee said, prodding his prisoner along as the startled rifleman watched.

Yahzee wished his bag of tricks weren't so limited, but it would have to do—and it did.

Shortly they were out of the slit-trench triggerman's view, and were near the high point of the incline, an outcropping of rock, sprouting a whiptail antenna. In lulls between rounds of gunfire and pounding shells a more subtle sound could be made out: the crackle of static . . . and Japanese voices, wafting up from a crevice in a gentle echo.

The scout and his prisoner—the former with bayonet nudging the latter, whose hands were again high—closed in on the radio position, a two-man crew with a heavy, barely portable radio, and an officer with sword-on-hip supervising, their outcropping open to the world on one side.

The officer, catching movement out of the corner of an eye, looked up and watched as the apparent Japanese soldier and his captive moved in their direction, closing the distance quickly. A hand on his sword, the officer began to rise . . .

. . . which Enders saw, and whispered back to Yahzee: "Now."

But this time Yahzee's response time was less than stellar: he was to whip that rifle around and fire away at the Japs . . . that was what he and Enders had agreed would happen . . . but the Navajo, blood draining from his face, was learning that working a radio was one thing, and killing point-blank another. . . .

In the meantime, that Jap officer seemed to sense something awry, and spat orders to his men, who were abandoning their radio duties to reach for their rifles.

"Fucking do it, Yahzee!"

But the codetalker couldn't make himself squeeze the trigger.

The officer's hand was on his holstered pistol, now, and Enders reared back, grabbing his own .45 out of Yahzee's belt, and blasting away as he fell backward, a head shot taking the officer out in a spray of red mist, dropping one of the crew with a fatal sucking chest wound.

But that last Jap had his rifle in his hands, with a clean shot at Enders. . . .

Yahzee leapt forward, lunging with the bayonet, impaling the startled soldier, his blade deep in the man's chest, piercing something major enough to spray blood, spattering red war paint on Yahzee's pale face.

The codetalker watched in silent horror as the Japanese soldier, his eyes pleading, flailed and squirmed on the end of the bayonet, a fish on a hook. Yahzee stared back at the man, whose high-cheekboned, bronzed face might have belonged to a cousin or brother.

Yahzee drew back, yanking the blade free, and the soldier stumbled onto the rocky ground, falling on his back, looking up at his assailant, gurgling, drowning in his own blood . . . finally, mercifully, dying.

And the Indian looked at the blood on his blade, and at the man at his feet . . . and his eyes stayed there, locked on the corpse he'd created, a corpse looking back at him with wide dead eyes. Were evil spirits rising, even now?

"Yahzee!"

The codetalker did not respond to his bodyguard's voice.

"Look at me, goddamnit."

Somehow Yahzee managed to pull his eyes off the man he'd murdered. Then he realized Enders had hold of him, was shaking him. . . .

"Listen to me—you did your job here. That's all. But that job ain't over—we got friends down the hill getting the shit blasted out of them, remember?"

Yahzee swallowed, nodded. Enders was right. Those 105s had to be re-directed.

The bodyguard's eyes were locked unblinkingly on his—and, somehow, Yahzee drew strength from that, as if the strong will of Joe Enders had seeped inside him.

As Enders dragged the bodies within the rock hollow for hiding, Yahzee worked the Japanese radio, speaking the Navajo code, and within minutes, big American guns were winching higher, before resuming their relentless pounding.

Only now their shells were rocketing over the

heads of Gunnery Sergeant Hjelmstad and the second squad, bearing down instead on that Japanese trenchline, where that suspicious sergeant was among the first to die when a volley of 105 shells blew their encampment, their trenches, and themselves to hell and gone.

Soon Enders and Yahzee—prisoner and captor no more, leaving that bulky Jap radio behind— were sprinting through the dust and debris, the exploding shells kicking up earth and dust, providing cover as they scurried desperately toward their own lines.

12

THE NEXT MORNING, AFTER A SOGGY NIGHT OF TROPICAL rainfall, the Marine Artillery base—a behind-the-lines array of tents and foxholes and trucks and dirt roads, a temporary town cut into a coconut grove—provided the setting for a rare day off the front for the men of Second Recon. Uniforms hung on branches, drying and airing out, and equipment matters could be tended to, as well as medical and other personal needs.

Off to one side, under a tree, Whitehorse was keeping a shirtless, reddish-tanned Ben Yahzee company as Yahzee got familiar with the replacement for the CR-300 field radio he'd lost in combat yesterday. His "new" radio was an old Army work-horse called the TBX—a clunky, eighty-pound affair consisting of two toolbox-like units, stacked and joined by a black cable. This was a battery-operated version—otherwise, handcranking would have turned codetalking into at least a two-man operation on just Yahzee's end—but the clunker was effective for long-range communications between inland fighting and ships at sea.

Sitting on an empty ammo crate next to the hole he'd dug himself—suitable for fighting or sleeping, easily converted to a grave, for that matter— Joe Enders tended to precious equipment of his own: his feet. He had just moved on to his left foot, a rather large and certainly well-tended, thoroughly scrubbed gunboat . . . as was the equally pampered right one, which (toes and all) had been returned to its boondocker. Now the left was receiving a Christmasy powdering of talcum, Enders rubbing the soothing stuff between his tender toes. The sergeant kept his feet as clean as his weaponry—no jungle rot for either, if he could help it.

The rumble of a Jeep rolling in turned a few heads, but most of these men, like Enders and Whitehorse, were busy. Hjelmstad, on his way somewhere, was the first to notice the emblem on the vehicle, and the full-bird colonel and his adjutant being chauffeured in to the base.

The gunnery sergeant called, "Yah-ten-hut!" and everybody in the general area scrambled to attention, including Whitehorse and Yahzee, though they were a ways away.

Enders sighed, irritated at having his hygiene interrupted, and got to his feet, only one of which was shod.

The colonel—a slender, weathered-looking, crisply uniformed man in his early forties—climbed out of the Jeep, throwing a salute at the men, and put them at ease.

To the group, he said, "I'm looking for a Sergeant Enders. . . ."

His adjutant, a slightly smaller, younger version of himself, handed forward a pad for the colonel's reference.

"Joseph F.," the colonel added.

Hjelmstad was about to answer, but Enders—embarrassed at being caught, as the nursery rhyme said, with one shoe off and one shoe on—was only a few yards away, and raised a hand and called out, "Here, sir!"

The colonel looked the sergeant up and down, noting the white-powdered bare foot. Then he said, "Get over here, Sergeant . . . with both boots."

Moving as he juggled with his boondocker, Enders jammed his left foot in, hell with socks, and got awkwardly over there.

Always uneasy about being singled out, Enders stood while the colonel checked the pad the adjutant had handed him.

"Report says you went above and beyond, yesterday."

". . . Sir?"

"Friendly fire incident. This is the second commendation you've been recommended for in two days, Sergeant. That's a distinction no other man on this island can claim."

Enders said nothing.

"Anyway, Command concurs with this commendation, and there's no sense you waiting for all the formalities to work themselves out."

"Sir?"

"Not when I have one of these handy." The colonel reached out toward the adjutant, without looking at the man, who filled the officer's palm with a Silver Star.

Enders felt sick.

The colonel was pinning the thing on him, having a little trouble, saying, "Congratulations, Sergeant Enders. Your effort, behind enemy lines, saved Marine lives yesterday."

Enders swallowed and said, "I, uh, wasn't alone in that effort, sir."

"Sergeant?"

He nodded toward Yahzee, who was still over with Whitehorse checking out that TBX, both codetalkers looking over at the colonel and Enders, but just out of earshot.

The colonel glanced toward Yahzee, but did not

acknowledge him. Instead, he said to Enders, "Oh, yes—your Indian codetalker. Posed as a Jap."

"That's right, sir. The plan, the tactics, that was all his idea, sir."

"Funny," the colonel said, and chuckled. "These codetalkers have been captured by our own people several times now, mistaken for the enemy. Happened twice on Guadalcanal. This is the first time the Navajo resemblance to Japs has paid off."

"Begging the colonel's pardon, Navajo is a white man's word. That Marine is of the Dineeh, of the Bitter Water people, born for the Towering House Clan."

"Of course . . . Dineeh. Towering House. I'll remember that."

But Enders could tell the colonel had already forgotten.

Then the adjutant was holding open the Jeep door for the colonel, who said, "You tell your codetalker he did good, too." Then the colonel hiked his volume and called out, "All of you men—keep up the good work!"

And the colonel drove away, to safety, and Enders knew the officer hadn't given the slightest consideration to presenting Ben Yahzee with a medal.

Enders, embarrassed—almost ashamed, when Yahzee took a moment away from checking out the radio to grin and wave at him, obviously aware his bodyguard had been commended—limped over to his crate to sit back down and take off his boot and get his sock on.

He was in the process when Chick, Pappas, Harrigan and several other guys came around to slap him on the back and give him shit and check out the shiny sliver of silver pinned to his dungaree shirt.

Late that afternoon, under an overcast, threatening sky that draped the makeshift base in blue shadows, Charlie Whitehorse was off by himself, sitting on an artillery crate, playing his wooden flute. The breathy, yet full-bodied, deep tones conspired to present a spare yet haunting melody that made Pete Anderson—coming up to join his codetalker, bearing a couple warm Cokes—smile with appreciation.

"That's real nice, Charlie," he said. "You teach yourself to play that thing?"

"Yes and no. My father played one of these. He didn't teach me, but I watched."

"Best way to learn, sometimes."

"Yeah—you can't beat 'em, join 'em."

"You can say that again." Anderson pulled up a crate and sat and dug his harmonica out of the breast pocket of his USMC dungaree shirt. "My pop played one of these—he gave me this. I used to play this little tune and it would bring the pigs right in . . . for feeding?"

"I don't suppose it's hard getting pigs to come in to eat."

"No. I admit as much. I'm okay on this thing, and you're damn good on yours—with our dads handing the instruments down and all, you and me a couple of farm boys. . . . We were born to play together."

Whitehorse swigged some Coke. "Then how come we sound like shit?"

They had already tried to play duets, as early as back at Camp Tarawa—the results inevitably a cross-cultural cluster fuck.

Anderson shrugged, blew a few melancholy notes. "I don't know—damn harmonicas are stuck in one key, maybe that's why. Look, let's try something different. . . . You go ahead and start, Charlie."

And Whitehorse—who by now was just humoring his bodyguard—started in on a Dineeh tune, while Anderson did his best to slide in, the results a dissonant disaster. They kept trying, though even the sky seemed to disapprove, thunder rolling, wind whipping up.

But, to the dismay of any within hearing distance, the two friends kept at it, Whitehorse putting up with, Anderson searching for, that perfect blend, a harmony that would echo Anderson's friendship with the man he was sworn, if necessary, to kill.

As dusk was turning into night, under a sky that was already dark enough to pass for midnight, Ben

Yahzee—in his rain-protective poncho—pushed against wind that was thinking about turning into a full-blown squall, heading through the drifting shadows and leaning blades of tall grass, angling toward the Marine perimeter. He had seen Enders lope off this way, and could tell something was bothering his bodyguard . . . even more than usual, though the hostility between them seemed now a thing of the past.

Joe Enders sat in his tee shirt, alone, leaning back up against a monkeypod tree, drinking from a small ceramic bottle. To Yahzee, his bodyguard looked at least a little drunk.

The sky was black now, the wind howling and rustling the trees, a grumble of thunder threatening rain.

From under his poncho, Yahzee withdrew a letter. "You seem to make a point of missing mail call, Enders."

The eyes that looked back at Yahzee were glassy. "Do I?"

Yahzee sniffed the letter's subtle perfume. "Smells like you made the right kind of friends, back in Hawaii. . . ."

Enders reached up and grabbed the letter out of Yahzee's hands, like a kid taking back a toy he didn't want to share; but then he just tossed the letter from Paradise Cove next to him, on the grassy ground . . . unopened.

A gust snatched the letter and sent it fluttering away; but, quick as the wind itself, Yahzee ran and stamped a boondocker down on it, taking a prisoner. He picked the letter up and walked back to the tree and knelt near Enders, who looked over at him curiously.

Yahzee unzipped Enders's knapsack and stuffed the letter inside.

"Just help yourself," Enders said.

On his haunches, Yahzee was zipping the bag back up. "My mother says, if somebody takes the time to write you a letter, least you can do is read it."

"Always do what your mama says?"

Yahzee nodded, stood, and turned, walking into that damn wind, which slowed him down—otherwise, he might not have heard Enders call out to him.

"Your mama let a big boy like you take a drink?"

Yahzee glanced back at Enders. "No. She takes an anti-firewater stand."

"Does she, now?"

". . . But I don't see her around here, anywhere."

Within moments Yahzee was sitting next to Enders under the monkeypod, wind ruffling its feathery leaves, riffling its crimson-stamined flowers, and the Indian accepted a small ceramic bottle of his own, a gift from Enders.

Yahzee sniffed the mouth of the little bottle. "What is this stuff?"

"It ain't chianti, but it'll do."

"Is this . . . sake?"

Enders nodded; it seemed to take great effort. "Good old rice wine . . . Jap sake."

Yahzee took a sip; it was strong, warm going down, turning hot. He liked it just fine.

"Need a fresh one," Enders said, having finished his bottle, and he reached back around the trunk of the monkeypod; this too took considerable effort.

Already feeling a buzz, Yahzee asked, "How much of this joy juice have you got, anyway?"

But Enders didn't seem to hear him, still leaned over, reaching around the tree.

When Enders had found his new bottle, and was sitting there removing the cork, Yahzee said, "You got a little trouble with that left ear, don't you?"

"No big deal. Some inner ear thing—throws my balance off, sometimes."

Back at Camp Tarawa, Charlie Whitehorse had told Yahzee that Enders had a hearing problem, but Yahzee had shrugged it off. But Whitehorse had insisted part of Enders's loner inclination came from the aloneness a person with poor hearing experiences.

Enders, perhaps wanting to change the subject, raised his little ceramic bottle. "You did good, Yahzee . . . up on that hill."

"Shit. I froze again."

"Jus' for a second. Everybody in combat has

things to get past . . . but you come through fine. Saved my raggedy ass."

"Yeah. . . ." And Yahzee grinned, maybe a little drunk himself. "Yeah, I did, didn't I?"

And they clinked their little bottles together. Drank together—though Enders drank longer, more deeply. Yahzee was pleased to find his bodyguard loosening up, finally, even if it had taken Jap joy juice to do it . . . only now Enders was staring off blankly, something troubled in the glassy eyes.

Yahzee followed the bodyguard's brooding gaze through the tall grass and the tropical trees to a small clearing nearby where another makeshift cemetery had been established, a row of rifles jammed into the earth, silenced weapons wearing empty helmets. . . .

Enders swigged sake, staring down at something in his palm: a medal . . . a Silver Star. His tunic, Yahzee noted, was already ripped a bit, from where he'd torn the medal off. How long had Enders been sitting here, drinking, under a dark growling sky, considering that hunk of silver, staring at those graves?

"Why don't you take this?" Enders asked, holding out the medal.

"You can't give me your medal . . ."

"Whole damn thing was your idea."

"Naw, it's got your name on it."

Enders stared at the Silver Star, grunted a non-laugh. "This is my second one, you know."

"Really?"

"Oh yeah—think I'll file it with the rest of my collection."

And he drew his arm back and threw the thing, threw it hard, the medal winging toward the fresh graves, landing somewhere in the near, tall grass.

Yahzee looked toward where Enders had hurled the medal, then said, softly, "What was the other one for?"

"For not dying. . . . Of course, fifteen guys in that particular battle got their own medals, too. They got theirs *for* dying. . . . Kinda doesn't make much sense, does it?"

Ender gulped some sake and leaned back against the tree and looked up at branches swaying in the wind, barely visible against the black sky. Leaves made brittle music.

Yahzee said nothing. He could sense Enders wanted to talk, but he didn't prod the man. Just shared the night and its sounds with him.

Finally Enders began to speak, and described a terrible battle on a beach on Guadalcanal. Yahzee just listened, as Enders spoke, interspersing the occasional chug of sake, as distant artillery fire joined the jungle night sounds, flashing white like lightning.

"Every man under my command was my friend . . . trusted me . . . and then they begged me to pull back, give it up, but I wouldn't. I followed orders. And you know what? Not one of them made it off that beach alive . . . wait, one did . . . one sorry son of a bitch made it . . . and you're lookin' at him."

Yahzee said nothing.

"That's how I won the Silver Star." Ender laughed but it didn't have anything to do with the usual reasons for laughing. Then he fell into a silence, half-brooding, half-drunken.

"Joe . . . Joe, what were their names?"

"Names?"

"It might help. Might be good to tell a story about these guys . . . who they were . . . what they were like."

"What the hell for?"

"To honor their memory . . . funny. That's something your people have given us, changed about us, my people . . . 'cause of this war."

"What do you mean?"

"Well . . . I told you about our attitudes toward death. The dangers, the evil spirits. . . . But we saw when the bodies of white soldiers were brought home, the dead were honored, buried with ceremonies of remembrance and love. Why should Navajos been denied such honor? And this . . . question of prestige, it broke the ancient taboos."

"Yeah?"

Yahzee nodded. "Photographs of deceased sons and brothers, who died in this war, they're displayed on mantels in homes, now. Remembered . . . honored. . . . Remembering your friends honors them, Joe. Keeps them in your mind and heart in a good way. . . . Their deaths weren't your fault, you were following orders, like any good Marine."

"Oh, I'm a good Marine, all right. One grade-A fucking leatherneck." And Enders stared right at Yahzee, and despite the glassy-eyed drunkenness in those eyes, the gaze was a piercing, terrible one. "Why do you think they gave me this shit detail?"

Enders downed the last of the rice wine and tossed the bottle away and got to his feet, leaning against the tree, the sake making rubber bands out of his legs.

Watching Enders stagger off, Yahzee felt a deep sense of connection to this man who so stubbornly shunned such human connections—the Indian remembered the moment he had looked in the dying Jap's face and thought that the poor bastard could have been his brother . . . but now he knew, now in some deep, even mystical manner, he understood that this tortured Anglo hero, stumbling into the night, was his real brother . . . as much as Charlie Whitehorse or even his real kin. . . .

Enders was having no such revelation. Fucked

up on sake, he was stumbling toward base, the ground damp, slippery, the trees around him turning grotesquely demonic, transforming the tough Marine into Snow White lost in the forest. Vines blowing in the growing wind seemed to reach out for him, their tickles like slaps, and he tottered, fumbling for his K-bar, got it, and began slashing at the vines, as if they were the enemy, as if he were fleeing some terrible bloody battlefield but his legs wouldn't work right for him, and the sounds inside his brain overwhelmed anything his ears might report, filling his head with the obscene brouhaha of combat, Guadalcanal again rising up to consume his haunted mind. . . .

He pushed ahead, to no avail: the tropical world around him began to spin, and what little sense of balance he had left slipped away, as he pitched forward, landing hard on the rocky earth, banging his left ear.

Ben Yahzee ran to his friend, leaned down over his barely conscious bodyguard, and was horrified to see blood oozing from that damaged ear.

"Jesus, Joe—you're bleeding! We gotta get you a corpsman. . . ."

Enders, tossing and turning as if caught in another nightmare, stared at the codetalker, and his confusion faded to anger. "No! Fuck no . . . I don't need no corpsman, just get me back to my damn hole, you hear? Get me back to my hole!"

And somehow Yahzee managed it, drunk-walking Enders across the jungle terrain, navigating the whipping wind, until they were in the city of tents and fox holes, everyone but a few guards asleep.

Breathing hard now, Yahzee set Enders down as gently, and as quietly, as he could, into the depression of the shallow gravelike hole. What little consciousness remained sputtered out as Enders's form hit mother earth.

For a moment Yahzee stood there, hands on his knees, catching his breath—hauling that bodyguard across camp had been harder than lugging a TBX. Then he stretched, extending those weary muscles of his, and looked down with satisfaction and some affection at Enders sleeping it off, his breathing even.

Yet even in sleep the bodyguard's face wore trouble lines, brow furrowed.

Checking to see if privacy would allow what he had in mind—and seeing sleeping Marines bivouacked all around—Yahzee skulked off and came back with a small charred piece of wood, the tip of which he rubbed into one palm, the fingers of his other hands dipping in to the ash, like a female about to apply make-up to herself.

But Yahzee applied the black powder, gently, to the sleeping Enders's forehead, a smear of ash—if anybody needed the Evil Way ceremony, it was this self-proclaimed "sorry son of a bitch."

As Yahzee was about to apply a second streak of

black, Enders's hand flew out and gripped the Indian's wrist, hard as a vice.

"Hey—I ain't *that* fuckin' drunk."

Startled, Yahzee drew back.

"You just . . . just cut that shit out. . . ."

And Enders settled back down, ready for another rough night of sleep, thanks to nightmares, wind and rain.

Yahzee waited a while, and then began smearing the ash onto his bodyguard's slumbering face, gentle as a mother, as determined as Enders himself.

When he was done, Yahzee found Enders's rain-slicker poncho and covered him up, like a child he was tucking in. Then he went to his own gravelike hole, and slept well.

13

THE NEXT DAYS WERE, UNTIL THE INCIDENT IN THE VILLAGE, blessedly free of intense combat. The Second Recon pushed ahead, staying hidden, noting the enemy's locations and movements and armaments, often with Enders and Yahzee on point, codetalking. Now and then, a sniper was spotted, and Chick Rogers got to fire his big BAR; but for the most part, duty consisted of such excitement as Hjelmstad's binoculars taking in enemy armor hidden under camouflage netting.

The terrain represented everything American soldiers had come to despise about the Pacific island war: swamps, sugarcane fields, jungle-draped mountains, steep ravines, and plenty of caves for the Japs to use as bunkers or for artillery positions. Battle had been slowed by the unremitting rain (sometimes lasting two minutes, sometimes two hours), though fighting did continue, as the Second Marines made use of the information their recon team was providing, and back on the warboard at the base map, little rising sun flags got pushed back, as the Japanese positions worsened in what was anything but a game.

Quiet moments occurred, Harrigan lighting up a cigarette under a monkeypod tree—as opposed to torching some poor SOB in a slit trench—taking five with the boys, but just five: Hjelmstad was always knocking on somebody's helmet, reminding them there was a war on, getting the squad moving.

Still, Joe Enders had found a more peaceful center, after his sake-soaked communion with his codetalker. At day's end, a blazing tropical sun setting through humid shimmer, he could sit in the jungle under a tree and study the natural beauty, focus on spores, tiny seed pods, insects, that world within this world that cared nothing about the petty conflicts of humans. He found himself taken with the throaty loveliness of Whitehorse's flute-playing, haunting tunes that seemed at once foreign and very American. And he would sit at sundown and read and re-read Rita's letters. . . .

They were chatty, upbeat yet melancholy missives. "Papers say our boys are doing great, but I don't think the reporters have been around to Kaneohe Bay Naval Hospital." She professed to avoid thinking about him, and what he might be doing, though admitted lying in bed wondering about what his day had been like, and where he slept. . . .

He actually wished he could write back to her—she said it drove her crazy, not knowing if he was reading these letters . . . were they even reaching him?

And she made a confession: "I didn't wish on that star that you'd be less of a horse's patoot, not really. . . . I wished you would come home to me, alive and not in need of me as nurse. Just as your girl. . . ."

And, walking down overgrown jungle paths, wind rustling through the canopy, these men from this part of America and that one gradually learned about each other not just as soldiers, but as men . . . guys with plans for the future: Anderson scheming to combine his father's strawberries with something called yogurt, a "surefire moneymaker if America would just develop a goddamn taste for the slimy stuff"; Whitehorse looking forward to returning to his sheep, his family (according to Yahzee) owning "the largest flock in the Four Corners area"; cab-driver Pappas dreaming of "a whole stinking fleet of taxis," after which he would visit the motherland and buy a villa "on the cliffs of Santorini"; Chick thinking about making a career out of the Marines (which earned him catcalls and much shit); and Harrigan just wanting to finish college, where he seemed to be majoring in coeds.

Yahzee wanted to finish college, too, but his intention was to teach.

"Teach?" Anderson had asked, as they trooped along, trying to avoid the occasional mud holes. "What, bring a little something of the outside world back to the reservation?"

"More like bring the reservation to the outside world. I'm hoping to teach college—American history."

Chick, who was wearing a bandage on his temple from a shrapnel scrape, guffawed and said, "Yeah, just what we need—Yahzee here, teachin' white boys about Custer's last stand."

"I was thinking more Kit Carson," Yahzee said, "and the Long Walk—ever read about that, Chick?"

Of course Chick—who hadn't read much of anything, except maybe the *Police Gazette* or crime comics—did not reply.

And when Yahzee asked Enders what he planned after the war, Enders was surprised to discover he hadn't given it much thought.

"Well you should, Joe," Yahzee said. "This war won't be here forever."

But Enders knew that for many of them, the war would be forever—that the dreams and yearnings these men were expressing would have seemed mundane before tours in places like Guadalcanal and Saipan. Now such plans seemed like pie in the sky. Why think about tomorrow, when surviving today was at such question?

Right now, the Marines of Second Recon were trudging toward the remains of a bombed-out village, skeletal structures visible beyond a Japanese torri gateway, one of those tall, two-pillared affairs with upsweeping crown so often built as the approach to a Shinto shrine.

The village itself—which had been inhabited by both Japanese and laborers consisting of Koreans and local natives, Chamarros, who had been working in the nearby sugarcane fields and processing plants—was an array of crumbling corrugated buildings and wooden huts; the smokestacks of bombed-out sugar refineries shared the sky with coconut palms. A small thriving community had become a ghost town, silent, eerie, just another casualty of war.

As the Marines moved warily through the gate, dangling ornaments clinking like off-key wind chimes, they thumbed off the safeties of their weapons. From ravaged homes and buildings, eyes peered out at them, gazes you could feel, like clammy air.

Gunnery Sergeant Hjelmstad signaled his Marines to split up and search the devastated village, and as Second Recon moved carefully through, rifles and machine guns and flame throwers at the ready, a ragtag, dazed welcoming committee drifted out of here and there like shell-shocked ghosts—Chamorran villagers, dusky natives, disheveled, dirty in tattered clothing and bare feet (the Koreans would be hiding, afraid to be misidentified as Japanese). Someplace a baby cried while elsewhere a goat bleated, as if communicating their shared misery.

Across the courtyard Enders could see a village woman in rags hurrying with a young boy, a bandage wrapped around the child's head, and then ducking into a half blown-to-shit warehouse building, obviously terrified. He was hardened to the sights of war—the corpses of the enemy and even those of his own cause; but these innocent bystanders, who happened to live in the midst of somebody else's conflict . . . that filled him with a sick hollow feeling.

When the village had been secured, and a command post installed, the second squad took a break, while the first squad went on patrol, with Harrigan and his flamethrower pressed in to duty. Anderson and Whitehorse took advantage of the lull for another of their impromptu, and thus far entirely unproductive, rehearsal sessions, this one conducted in the remains of a Buddhist shrine.

Sitting next to Whitehorse on a bench that Anderson assumed was the Buddhist equivalent of a pew, the pair did their best to harmonize, Navajo flute and all-American harmonica, coming up with the usual discord. Whitehorse fell out first, but then Anderson gave up the ghost, as well.

"Maybe I was all wet," Anderson said.

"In this climate, that's no surprise."

"Yeah . . . shit." Anderson hung his head, shook it glumly. "Maybe we aren't meant to play together. Like I said, these things are stuck in one key . . ."

They sat silently for a few moments, and then Whitehorse said, evenly, "I used to play for the sheep."

"Huh? You mean, like I used to play for the pigs?"

The moon-faced Indian nodded. "Sheep ain't hard to make come in to eat, either."

Anderson's frustration was gone; he was grinning now. "No shit, just like me and the pigs . . . you and the sheep. . . . You never did nothin' else with those sheep, did you, Charlie?"

Whitehorse surrendered one of his rare grins. "No, Ox—I just played for 'em. How about you and the pigs?"

Anderson raised his eyebrows and smiled one-sidedly. "Well, I been with a few pigs in my time, just not on the farm."

Whitehorse chuckled. "What the hell—why don't you play for the pigs, and I'll play for the sheep . . . see what happens."

Anderson, his enthusiasm back, raised his harmonica and started in on a countrified ditty, while Whitehorse lifted his flute and a lilting, typically haunting native tune emerged . . . music as different as Whitehorse and Anderson, but also like the Marines, somehow kindred. Harmony happened, at once. . . .

It wasn't perfect—after a fine start, a few notes didn't merge, and adjustments had to be made. Whitehorse paused, letting Anderson slide ahead a few bars, then the Indian came in and the harmony blossomed, the duet sang, music red and white (and a little blue) blending perfectly in a simple melody that sounded (as Anderson said afterward) "pretty damn good."

Codetalker Ben Yahzee had slipped away from his bodyguard, and now had lost track of him. He tried the warehouse, where he'd noticed Enders's attention had been attracted when they tramped into town; and, as he moved down the wooden sidewalk, a noise in the ruined building drew him to a window.

Through a tear in the rice-paper, Yahzee could see Enders kneeling beside a village boy. The lad was dark as a Navajo, and crouched in pain, a blood-stained rag around his head. The boy seemed suspicious—though he made no attempt to flee—as the American soldier reached in his shirt pocket, and withdrew a vial.

Though they had never spoken of it, not directly, Yahzee knew the vial contained pain killers, the tablets Enders would resort to when his damaged ear was really bothering him. Right now Enders was holding out a hand with one of those tablets in his palm, and with his other hand offering his canteen of water.

The little boy studied Enders for the longest time, searching the man's eyes; finally the child decided the Marine meant only to help, and reached out and took the tablet, and swallowed it with a gulp of water from the canteen Enders held for him.

When Yahzee entered the warehouse, the boy had moved to the rear of the warehouse, rejoining his frightened mother. Enders stood at the table, its surface covered with flour remaining from rolling out dough; mother and son lived here, their home probably blasted to bits by one side or other. A few Catholic icons—a statue of Mary, a cross—sat here and there on windowsills, overseeing scraps of battered, scavenged furniture.

Enders—who'd been absent-mindedly drawing something in the flour on the table—looked up at Yahzee and said, "Where the hell have you been?"

"*Na-nil-in*," Yahzee said.

"What's that code for?"

"For something private . . . personal. . . . I had to take a piss, and didn't figure you needed to watch."

"Hey—check with me before you go wandering off . . . that's the drill."

But the bite was out of Enders's words by now; they were friends and the dynamic had changed.

Yahzee looked at the image Enders was drawing in the flour: not a bad representation of a church, the exterior of a Catholic church.

"You Catholic?" Yahzee asked.

"Used to be. . . . Had to make these people comfortable with me." He nodded toward the mother and son, at the rear, the mom cradling the now comfortable boy in her lap. "They're Catholics, is the point."

"I thought these people were Buddhists or something."

"Just the Japs. The missionaries got to these natives, a long time ago."

"Tell me about it," Yahzee said. "I was raised Catholic myself—mission school on the reservation."

Enders smirked. "Hey, I'm a veteran of the good nuns at Archbishop Keenan. Kind of lost interest in the faith, the penguins rapping my head every time I mouthed off."

Yahzee nodded. "Fathers didn't like us talking Navajo at mass, and when I forgot one Sunday, they chained me to the radiator in the basement for two nights."

"Ain't Christianity wonderful?"

"Think I was about eight years old."

Enders snorted. "When I was eight they confirmed me, anointed me with holy water—"

"Oil."

"Huh?"

"You get confirmed with oil, not holy water."

"Whatever the hell. Anyway, they told me I was a Soldier of Christ." Enders gestured toward his khakis. "Guess somewhere along the line I switched units."

"Me, too. Question is—did we switch sides?"

Enders thought about that for a second, then he said, "Well, the white man sure wants you to talk Navajo now."

The two friends sat at the flour-covered table and chewed the fat for a good fifteen minutes, the facades, the barriers finally, completely, down. Yahzee invited Enders to come visit him at Monument Valley after the war, to do things you couldn't do in the Corps, like ride horses, and eat fry-bread, do some hunting. . . .

"Well," Yahzee said, eyeing Enders's Thompson on the table next to the Catholic church drawn in flour, "maybe we'll pass on the hunting."

Enders smiled a little. "Kind of a long drive, from Philly to Arizona."

"It'd be worth it. You could meet my son . . . and he could meet Joe Enders, the guy Uncle Sam assigned to watch over his pop's scrawny ass."

Enders still wore the small smile; after a moment he said, "I bet you're a hell of father, Ben."

Hearing Enders call him "Ben" startled Yahzee; it was the first time . . . and, for some reason, the friendly familiarity of it touched the Navajo deeply.

"What kind of name is Enders, anyway?" Yahzee asked.

"Italian. Endrolfini, before some asshole at Ellis Island got hold of it."

A noncommissioned officer from another outfit poked his head in the warehouse door, a little out of breath; he'd obviously been looking around for them, or anyway, one of them: he spoke to Yahzee. "Captain needs to code a message back to the CP— you the Indian?"

Yahzee looked at Enders with an arched eyebrow and Enders laughed and shook his head.

"Yeah," Yahzee said, getting up, "I'm the Indian."

And the codetalker left the NCO, not seeing his bodyguard's troubled expression, Enders sitting there, staring at the image of the church in the flour.

Then Enders erased the image with his palm, and got quickly up, and went out onto the street of the dead village. Yahzee was not in sight, but Sergeant Fortino was leading the men of the first squad back in after patrol, Harrigan with them.

As Enders passed by, he was vaguely aware of Harrigan—peeling off the first squad to rejoin the second—pausing in the intersecting street to offer a little native girl in rags some candy.

"Here, take it," Harrigan was saying, leaning down, "it's pogey bait—chocolate . . . it's good."

The girl hesitated, but then snatched the candy bar from Harrigan and stuffed it in her mouth, whole, chewed a little and swallowed. Then she held out her tiny, dirty hand for more.

Harrigan, shaking his head, grinning, got out another candy bar and broke off a smaller piece this time. He gave it to her, cautioning, "Now you gotta *chew* this time," and he mimicked the motions.

In the meantime, Enders had approached the mostly blown-apart building—had it been a cafe?—where the Second Recon command post had been established. Hjelmstad and the rest of second squad were there, relaxing, sitting here and there, leaning against walls, generally goofing off.

The gunnery sergeant was trying to open a tin of fish, from which the foul stench of lye emanated. He was having trouble with the key and not really getting anywhere.

When Enders approached, Hjelmstad paused in his effort and asked, "Ever had lutefisk, Joe?"

"Can't say I have, Gunny. I need to talk to you."

"Got this in the mail today. You ain't lived till you had lutefisk."

"I need out, Gunny."

Hjelmstad looked up, sharply. "What are you talkin' about?"

Enders could feel the muscles in his jaw tensing, trembling. "This detail—this duty. I can't perform it anymore."

Hjelmstad stared at him, as if trying to see if Enders were making some bad joke; then he said,

"You been doin' just fine till now—winning medals left and right."

Enders stiffened, and put formality into his voice. "Gunny, I'm requesting mast with battalion commander."

"Yeah?"

"I want out."

"You want out? Join the fucking club. You, me and every mother's son wants out of this war—my cousin in Oslo wanted out, too, but instead the Nazis lined him and a dozen of his buddies up against the wall, and cut 'em down like so much rotten wheat."

"I didn't say I wanted out of the war. I didn't say I wanted out of combat. You're not hearing me, Gunny. . . ."

"Oh, I'm hearing you just fine. Now you listen to me: there's a goddamn war going on, worldwide if you haven't noticed, and it ain't being waged on your wants and your schedule. Now, go catch some sack-time and get over this shit. . . . That's an order!"

Hjelmstad, having given a that's-that speech, returned his attention to the bent key on the tin of lutefisk; he did not expect Enders's hand to grip his wrist like a vise, and whirl him back, the fish from home flying.

"Goddamnit, Gunny, listen to me!" And Enders had lifted the superior officer off the ground, grabbing him by the front of his tunic. "I can no longer perform my duty!"

Hjelmstad—shocked—just stared at Enders, hanging from the man's fists like a suit of empty clothes. And the men of the second squad, in the nearby background—who had gradually been picking up on this strained conversation—now looked on in wide-eyed, gape-jawed amazement. The bravest man in the squad had lost his marbles, gone well and truly Asiatic. . . .

Enders swallowed, embarrassed, humiliated by his loss of control, let Hjelmstad go, and stood there, shoulders slumped, waiting for his reprimand.

It never came: small arms fire interrupted and took precedence.

Harrigan, out in the street sharing candy with the child, had caught a bullet in the calf, and was toppling to the dusty pavement, even as a fusillade of gunfire ripped into the village, seeming to come from all directions, sending every man in the second squad diving for cover.

Only that child did not seek shelter—she stood frozen, terrified, staring at the wounded man with the candy bar in his hand.

14

ENDERS HAD HIS THOMPSON BLAZING BEFORE THE REST OF the squad could grab their weapons and join in; but within seconds, from behind the partial wall of their command post, the Marines were sending return fire toward the unseen enemy, and doing their best not to catch Harrigan or that frozen-in-the-crossfire child.

Reaching a hand back to try to stem the bleeding from his bullet-punctured calf, Harrigan—belly down on the street, looking like a human bug with the bulky flamethrower canisters on his back—was yelling at the girl, "Get out of here! Go!"

No matter how he yelled at her, or tried to wave her away, the girl didn't budge, just stood with bullets whizzing all around, and kept staring at Harrigan.

Enders thought he knew what this was about: Harrigan, in his other hand, still held that candy bar. . . .

Of the squad, Pappas, over by the doorway of the half-wall, was nearest to Harrigan and the child.

"She wants that fucking candy bar," Enders said to the Greek. Then he yelled to Harrigan: "She wants the pogey bait!"

Pappas, rifle blasting, scrambled out on the sidewalk, getting as close as he dared, and Harrigan tossed the chocolate bar toward him, Pappy catching it one-handed between M-1 rounds.

Enders had been right: the child ran after the candy, toward Pappas, who darted out to meet her, scooped her up, and carried her back behind the partial wall for cover.

Despite the onslaught of gunfire from either side, all of second squad heard the telltale metallic clank, and Enders and the rest paused in momentary shock: a bullet had ripped into one of those tanks strapped to Harrigan's back, gas streaming out. Doing a one-legged dance, risking rising up into the crossfire, Harrigan struggled to crawl out of the tanks.

The sound was surprisingly small, as explosions of recent days went: it only registered on Enders's good ear, in fact.

Nonetheless, the *ka-wooosh* was something

those who survived this day would never forget; nor—when the canisters went up in a terrible fireball, consuming Harrigan like the tip of match igniting—would they forget their friend's heart-rending shrieks of pain. That his death was relatively quick represented one small mercy in this unforgiving war.

Battle-hardened though he was, for several long moments Enders was as frozen as that dusky little girl had been, staring at the candy bar; the horror of it turned all of them pale, though no one could have known as much, as the faces of the second squad were painted orange by the flames.

As he glanced at the squad around him, Enders suddenly realized Yahzee had not returned from that communications errand he'd gone off on—hell, Enders wasn't even sure what squad Yahzee had gone off to codetalk for!

As firing resumed across the intersection where the charred remains of one of their own danced and crackled with flame, Enders yelled between rounds at Hjelmstad: "Where's first squad holed up?"

"Down by what's left of that Buddhist shrine," Hjelmstad said, using his .45, his twelve-gauge no good at this range. "Chick's down there, with 'em. . . ."

"I gotta get Yahzee," he said, with an apologetic glance to his gunnery sergeant. "My orders. . . ."

"Glad to see you following them," Hjelmstad

said, nodding his permission, as he snapped off rounds.

In the hilltop courtyard outside the Buddhist shrine, the first squad—Anderson and White-horse—was in the thick of it; this fire fight had already gone close quarters, with the handful of Marines taking cover behind partial walls, as Japs came pouring up the hillside, all around.

Chick—firing from behind a well, its circular shape aiding him in swiveling around as the enemy came from various directions—had picked off his share of the bastards. But now the Texan's BAR clicked on an empty chamber, and he hunkered down and was changing magazines when a rifle butt swung his way and clubbed him to the ground.

Stunned, Chick nonetheless recognized the cold round steel pressed on his neck as the kiss of a rifle barrel, and also knew the sound of the Jap cycling a rifle bolt signaled the last seconds of his life . . .

. . . but the next noise was not a rifle firing into him, rather a thud; something flopped down heavily right next to him . . . and Chick was staring into the open blank eyes of the soldier who, moments before, had been preparing to end the Texan's life. A bone-handled knife—a Navajo blade—protruded from the dead Jap's neck.

As he got up into firing position at the well,

Chick could see Whitehorse across the courtyard, using both hands to fire his M-1; but the Texan knew one of those hands had hurled the knife that had saved him . . . and he caught Whitehorse's eyes and the two men nodded and both went back to the war, Chick finally jamming in that new mag.

The cause here all but lost, Chick hauled ass back toward the command post, hoping to help the second squad out with his big BAR.

As Chick went one way, Enders was coming the other way a street over, running down the sidewalk, keeping his back to what walls existed in this already nearly decimated town, blowing enemy soldiers off their feet and into eternity with his roaring Thompson, its barrel hotter than hell as it breathed smoke and flame.

He spotted a Marine limping down the street, a trio of Japs closing in; was it Ben?

"Yahzee!" he yelled, ready to pitch in, but a shell exploded in the street—the artillery joining the small arms fire, now—and Enders was hurled through the air, just another chunk of debris. He did not see that poor Marine—who was not Yahzee—get chopped down by gunfire. Flung against bricks, his Thompson flying elsewhere, gone in the madness, Enders lost consciousness.

By this time, Chick had rejoined the second squad, hurling himself and his formidable weapon in alongside Hjelmstad behind half a wall.

"Thought maybe you could use this baby, Gunny," Chick said, patting the BAR.

Hjelmstad was loading up his twelve-gauge. "You came just in time to leave, Chick. . . . Pull back! *Pull back!*"

Back at the hilltop courtyard near the remains of that Buddhist temple, bodies were strewn everywhere, American and Japanese alike; but the landscape was crawling with Japs and only a few Americans remained—living ones, anyway.

Behind a crumbling excuse for a wall, Pete Anderson of Oxnard, California, was fighting alongside Navajo Charlie Whitehorse from Arizona with soldiers of Japan all around them; even in the midst of combat, Anderson's mind had time to scream at him: *the bastards can't be allowed to capture a codetalker. . . .*

A bullet ripped into Anderson, into his left side; it was like he'd been punched, staggering him.

"Son of a bitch," he said, and then he saw a Jap poised a few feet away, aiming right at Whitehorse, and Anderson knew, his mind calculated instantly, that their situation was hopeless, that he should allow that Jap to do what Anderson knew he himself could never do, and instead Anderson swung his Thompson around, and shot once—he was on his last magazine—and the Jap took the head shot with a jolt and a crimson splash, and lay down.

Whitehorse and Anderson exchanged split-second looks that somehow conveyed a lifetime of friendship, and another bullet ripped into Anderson, his right side this time. This time it hurt, hurt like hell, and the blinding pain sent him to his knees, battle ribbons of blood streaming from the two wounds. He saw a Jap closing in on Whitehorse, and he again raised that Tommy gun.

Whitehorse saw something else: another Jap rushing behind Anderson, with a samurai sword raised in sideways, executioner-style, sunlight gleaming off the well-polished blade, so close Whitehorse could see his own face in it, and the Navajo cried, "Ox!"

Anderson's eyes narrowed, but he never felt a thing, as the blade swung around and lopped his head right off. The last thing he heard—never dreaming his mind and body were separated—was Whitehorse shooting his M-1 at somebody who must have been coming up behind Anderson, and then blackness came.

As Hjelmstad and the second squad were retreating to safer ground, a dazed Enders dragged himself through streets littered with American and Japanese bodies, the little town barely visible through the battle dust, the firing, the shelling fallen silent, for now. A battle had been won on these devastated streets, and Enders had not been part of the prevailing side.

He called out for his codetalker, got no reply; still—his hearing even more screwed up than usual, after taking that ride, courtesy of an enemy shell—Sergeant Joe Enders slogged on, searching, even though the village around him, hell, the entire world, seemed strangely out of sync. . . .

Finally—his Thompson lost, his .45 empty and him with nothing to feed it—Enders stumbled up the slope and stepped through half a wall onto the Buddhist courtyard where the first squad had made its last stand, a holy place turned charnel house, strewn with bodies and body parts, Japanese and Marines alike. He almost stumbled over Sergeant Fortino, who lay beside a dead Jap—both men with bloody combat blades in hand.

Smoke and stirred dust floated, as Enders staggered through the brutal scene. Right now he didn't see any live Japs, but he heard Japanese; then he heard something else: *Yahzee*.

Yahzee's voice, crackling and remote and strange, cut through the drifting battle fog, and Enders moved toward it, quickly, keeping low, dropping down beside a well.

Maybe thirty yards away, he found a Navajo, all right: Whitehorse. Yahzee's voice crackled over the field radio next to big Charlie Whitehorse, sprawled there, breathing hard, bullet-riddled; the Indian could obviously hear Yahzee's pleading efforts, but he could not respond.

Next to the fallen Indian warrior, looking right at Enders, was Pete Anderson . . . or anyway, Pete Anderson's head.

Enders hadn't had time to process this latest

horror when more voices made themselves known through the haze of dust and smoke: not Navajo, not hardly . . . Japanese.

And it was more than just voices: gunshots. A handful of Japs were walking through the rubble, chatting, stepping over and around the casualties, and shooting any living Americans they came across, among the dead and dying.

Unarmed, Enders ducked down behind the well; he whispered: "Whitehorse!"

The Navajo—already reacting to the Japanese voices and the cracks of rifle fire—had reared up, some; now, hearing Enders, he tried to crawl toward the familiar voice. His bone-handed knife was in one hand, and—his legs not serving him— he used the blade to dig into the earth and pull his battered, bullet-bloody body along.

Enders watched aghast as the handful of soldiers reached Whitehorse, and one of them aimed his rifle down at the Indian. . . .

Japanese words—not bullets—cracked in the air, as a superior officer in round plastic-framed glasses and a cap with kepi walked into the midst of the casual executioners.

Enders could understand little Japanese; but he could read faces—and the gleeful face of this officer . . . an intelligence officer, no doubt—told the bodyguard that the man in the Tojo glasses understood who Whitehorse was.

Yahzee's voice, crackling over the field radio in

Navajo code, only made the kneeling officer smile, further confirming the man's awareness of the significance . . . the importance . . . of locating a codetalker, still alive.

Enders, his ears ringing, alone, unarmed, looked around in panic. All these dead Marines, flung as carelessly as if discarded . . . had they fought to their last round of ammo? Certainly some weapon had to remain, had to be within his reach. . . .

Then he saw it—half-buried by rubble, clutched in the hand of a Marine who had never got to use it: a grenade.

Enders scrambled to the body, plucked the grenade from limp fingers; this was good, but a gun would be better . . . he could save Whitehorse, then. . . . Only, when he looked up, Enders knew it was too late. They were dragging Whitehorse away, two soldiers being led by a self-satisfied intelligence officer who knew he had, held within the mind of one wounded prisoner, the information that could turn the tide of this war. . . .

Though no shells were dropping, Enders heard a pounding in his left ear, an ominous bass drum that seemed to underscore his lack of options. He fumbled with the pin, pulled it loose, and followed his orders, orders that Pete Anderson had not been able to obey.

Enders hurled the grenade.

He did not see, emerging from the smoke and drifting dust, another Navajo face, as Ben Yahzee—already struggling to focus in the haze—climbed to the hilltop only to see something he could not comprehend: Joe Enders throwing a grenade at Charlie Whitehorse.

And when the grenade bounced at his feet, Whitehorse—in the midst of his Japanese chaperons—looked down at the USMC-issue ordnance, forcing his numbed gaze to focus, then glanced back in one long last final moment at Joe Enders; their eyes met, locked.

Was it Enders's imagination, or maybe wishful thinking, that he saw understanding and acceptance in the unblinking eyes in that solemn moon face?

Yahzee screamed in protest and Whitehorse closed his eyes and the grenade exploded taking the Japs and the Navajo with it.

And when the smoke began to clear, Ben Yahzee stood staring unbelievingly at the empty place where his friend used to be. Then, when the disbelief faded, rage welled up, filled him, and he looked at Joe Enders—slump-shouldered, head lowered, but returning his gaze unflinchingly—and ran toward his so-called bodyguard.

Enders put up all the resistance of a tackling dummy when Yahzee, screaming in fury and sorrow, took him down hard, and the two rolled together down the hillside, taking a rough ride over rocks, tearing through brush.

When they finally landed, Yahzee was on top, swinging his fists, kneeing the bodyguard, even clawing at his face, the rage coming out in savage bursts—and Enders, the bigger, the tougher of the two, did nothing to defend himself.

They had spilled out into the flatter land, a battlefield strewn with bodies from both sides, an aboveground graveyard on which two of the corpses seemed to be struggling . . . or rather one corpse was pummeling another, the latter as seemingly dead as any of those around him.

Finally Yahzee, exhausted from this explosion of primal rage, yanked his .45 from its holster and shoved the snout against the side of Enders's bloodied, impassive face, near his right eye.

"Go ahead," Enders muttered. "Do it . . . I would."

Still on top of him, breathing hard, as if they were making love not war, Yahzee began to squeeze that trigger. . . . Then, trembling, the Indian's finger eased, though the gun barrel remained in place.

"*Na-nil-in,*" Enders said, his eyes half-lidded, woeful.

Yahzee just looked at him, .45 still pressed near the man's cheekbone.

"Something secret," Enders said, voice sandpaper rough, "confidential."

"What the hell are you talking about?"

"I'm talking about my orders, Ben." He let air out—sort of a sigh, almost a humorless laugh. "You codetalkers are important—but not as important as your code. If the Japs ever got hold of one of you boys, and your tongue got loosened . . . code's useless."

"What . . . what are you saying?"

"What you *think* I'm saying: I didn't have a choice, Ben. My orders aren't to protect you—I'm to protect the code."

Yahzee sensed somebody lunging at him, but didn't react fast enough, hands yanking him bodily off and away from Enders, knocking the gun from the Indian's fingertips, too.

And when Enders managed to sit up, spitting blood, woozy from the beating, he saw Pappas, standing behind Yahzee, his arms around him, gripping him, in a Greek bear hug.

Hjelmstad, striding over, wading through the bodies, said, "What the hell goes on here?"

Enders was on his feet.

Almost nose to nose with the bodyguard now, Hjelmstad demanded: "Well, Sergeant?"

Enders shrugged, which didn't hurt any more than having a tooth pulled. "Nothing's going on. . . . Pappy, let him go."

Yahzee had stopped squirming, but Pappas still looked skeptical, and turned to Hjelmstad, the ranking officer, for his opinion.

But Enders barked, "Let him fucking go!"

Pappas released his grip and stepped back, and Yahzee just stood there, glaring at Enders. Then he started up the hillside.

"Yahzee," Hjelmstad said, "where the hell you think you're goin'?"

The Navajo did not reply, just kept moving inexorably up the slope.

Hjelmstad shot Enders a look that demanded an explanation, but Enders just mumbled, "Gettin' his buddy's knife, most likely."

"Whitehorse?"

Enders nodded. "They got him, and Anderson, too."

"Jesus," the gunnery sergeant said. "First Harrigan, now those two."

But Enders wasn't listening: surrounded by Saipan's dead, he was studying the silhouette of his codetalker, Yahzee at first crouching, then standing, with the Navajo blade in hand.

15

On a hilltop granting him a view of the Pacific Ocean—a dark, brooding expanse almost merging with an equally dark, ominous afternoon sky— Ben Yahzee ignored the puffs of smoke and bursts of flame far below, indicating an island still embroiled in war. Sprinkling pollen from his leather pouch onto the earth, he knelt and paid homage to the Four Directions, and to his late friend, Charlie Whitehorse.

Then he rose and walked down the hill, putting his helmet on, rejoining the Second Recon, who were licking their wounds, counting their dead, and regrouping to get right back into the war.

Despite the heavy losses in that blown-out village, the big picture for Operation Forager was bright. The taking of Saipan—though a longer process than the brass had ever imagined—was well under way, the Marines pushing the Japanese toward the sea. As U.S. tanks rolled over the rough terrain, crushing an occasional enemy corpse under grinding steel tracks, supply trucks towed heavy artillery, while foot soldiers brought up the rear, what was left of Second Recon mixed in with a rifle squad of the Eighth Marines.

Joe Enders trudged down a well-rutted path, mud caked and brittle—despite the dark sky, no rain for a while—giving the thicket of green on either side a slow, ongoing scan for snipers. Chick Rogers—his gung-ho bravado worn away by too many days on this damned island—fell in alongside Enders.

"Got one of them homerolleds you could spare, Sarge?" the Texan asked. "I don't 'spose your spittle'll kill me." Chick had long since run out of chewing tobacco.

Enders nodded, fished out his tarnished cigarette box, opened it and let Chick help himself.

"Got a light, Joe?" Chick grinned goofily. "I usually chew this shit, y'know. . . ."

Without pausing in their march, Enders got out his Zippo, fired up Chick's smoke.

They walked a while, just two Marines clanking along in the pack. Then Chick asked, maybe a little too casually, "Heard you and your codetalker fell out, some."

"You could say that."

"I heard it was a pretty fair dust-up."

"Did you."

They walked some more, and—when it was clear Enders had nothing else to offer on this subject—Chick laughed, in a hollow, unamused way. "You know, ol' Whitehorse saved my Texas tail, back there. . . . Shoulda seen that redskin toss that knife. Never seen anything like it, this side of a circus."

Enders said nothing, still checking for snipers.

Chick was saying, "Wonder what ol' George Armstrong Custer would think about a buck like Whitehorse saving a longhorn like me? . . . I remember my gran'pappy sittin' on the porch, out on his farm . . . talkin' about Indians like they was goddamn gophers. He said him and his saddle pards used to get paid three bucks per ear."

". . . What?"

"For every comanche ear, they'd get three bucks."

"Hell of a way to make a dollar."

"Yeah . . . gets you thinkin'."

"Does it?"

Chick nodded. "You figure maybe in another fifty years, when this slice of hell is long behind us, we'll be sitting down with the Nips? Drinking sake, passin' around bowls of rice, shooting the shit?"

Enders gave him a sideways look.

Chick was lost in his speculation, his eyes big.

"And maybe the Japs'll be marching right with us, all of us going after somebody new's ass to kick."

Enders's eyebrows had climbed. "Corporal?"

"Yeah?"

"You're thinking so much, *my* brain's starting to hurt."

And Enders picked up his pace, leaving the Texan behind.

Chick—smiling to himself, shaking his head, chuckling as he took a slow drag on the home-rolled—realized this was a first: no one had ever accused him of thinking too much, before.

By sundown, the Second Recon was amid the company bivouacked behind the artillery, even as the 105mm howitzers continued to pummel the enemy, with one insistent boom after another. Bone-tired from pushing through this goddamn enemy-held jungle, the Eighth Marines sat on their packs, ate their C-rations and studied the setting sun, many of them wondering if that blazing ball could be the same one shining over their loved ones back home.

Just at the perimeter of camp, Ben Yahzee stood staring into his helmet, held in his two hands like a ball he'd caught, his eyes fastened upon the picture of his wife and son. The Indian sensed someone approaching, and somehow knew it was Enders, but did not even look up, much less turn.

"Thought I told you not to go traipsing off on

your own," Enders said, but the words had no bite, weariness had set in.

Looking up at the crimson sky, Yahzee said, "What's wrong, Joe? Afraid you can't hit a moving target?"

Enders stepped up beside his codetalker, casually lighting up a homerolled, not rising to the bait. "Red sky at night, sailor's delight."

"Too bad we ain't sailors."

Enders shrugged. "Marines are Navy men—just don't spread it around. Spoil a lot of good barroom fights."

Yahzee gazed down into his helmet. "Charlie blessed my boy in the Navajo way, the day George was born."

After a nod and a sigh, Enders said, "Charlie saved Chick's life today, did you know that?"

The Indian put the helmet on; he did not look at his bodyguard. "When Charlie wondered about 'cowboys watching Indians' back,' I thought he was just being Charlie."

"This isn't a white man, red man thing, Ben, and you know it."

Yahzee finally turned to look at Enders. "This is my fault, too."

"What?"

"Charlie didn't want to come to this white man's war, not at first."

". . . And you talked him into it?"

Yahzee nodded, swallowed thickly.

"Maybe you made a mistake," Enders said.

"Maybe we all did."

Enders shook his head. "Ben, you're a soldier—you're a Marine. You should understand this: I was following orders."

Yahzee smiled at the bodyguard, a terrible thing that had nothing to do with the usual reasons for smiling. "Of course you were, Joe. You're a good Marine—'one grade-A fucking leatherneck,' remember? . . . Why do you think they gave you this shit detail?"

And Yahzee stared at his bodyguard, for moments that seemed an eternity; and Enders did not like the new hardness in the Navajo's face, the cynicism—it was too much like looking in a mirror. . . .

Yahzee walked off; Enders did not follow.

Soon, however, they shared the proximity of their shrinking group—the remainder of first and second squad were now one—and Enders used his bayonet to open a tin of rations, not bothering with doctoring his chow with the usual pound of salt. With the hammering of howitzers an unsettling backdrop, he sat, alone, and ate the cold crap while Yahzee, keeping his distance, skipped chow entirely, busy wrapping twine around the handle of Whitehorse's knife. The bone had shattered in combat, and the repair was necessary.

Satisfied with the mended grip, Yahzee slid the weapon into another item of Whitehorse's that he'd inherited: a sheath, worn on the right calf.

Enders, pretending not to notice this, was startled when Pappas leaned in and nudged him out of his negative reverie.

"The Viking wants you," Pappy said.

Helmet off, Hjelmstad was sitting by himself on his pack, ammo-ing up, twelve-gauge on the ground beside him.

Enders stepped up and said, "You wanted to see me, Gunny?"

Hjelmstad didn't miss a beat as he inserted shotgun shells into a bandolier. "We got an early one, Enders—movin' out at 0700, full hour before the rest of the regiment."

As the two men spoke, those big guns kept blasting—the men of Second Recon might be resting between battles, but the war continued without them.

Enders asked, "Do we know what it's about?"

"Destination's that big chunk of rock out there." Hjelmstad nodded toward the mountain peak looming above the trees, foreboding in the haze of shelling—this was what the howitzers had been firing at. "That's Mount Tapotchau—highest point on the island."

"We take it," Enders said, nodding, "the island's ours."

"That's pretty much the thinkin' by those who are smarter than us, smart enough not to be in the middle of this shitstorm, anyway." He started in on a second bandolier. "Even so, the brass is nervous—expected more resistance."

"Which is where we come in. Recon."

"Yup. They want us to take a look-see over the other side of that glorified hill, in case we might spot something air surveillance couldn't . . . make sure Mr. Moto don't have nothin' wily up his sleeve."

"I saw all those movies—Mr. Moto *always* had something up his sleeve."

"Well, it's our job to find out what it is." The gunnery sergeant paused in his ammo effort to lock eyes with Enders. "Look—this is vital duty, and it's tied right in with you and that codetalker. Without him and his special skills, we—and by that I mean every Marine on this island—are well and truly fucked."

Enders said nothing.

"Joe, if there's some problem between you and Yahzee—best let me know."

Enders glanced across the camp at the Indian, who was preparing for sleep. Then he looked at Hjelmstad and shrugged. "No problem here, Gunny."

"Earlier today, seemed like there was. I have this vague memory of some asshole getting insubordinate."

A flush of shame rose up Enders's neck. "You have a right to tear these stripes off, Gunny. I won't say a word."

Hjelmstad merely smiled, shaking his head a little. "You're the best man on this island, Joe. I'm not going to be the man who turned a medal magnet like you into a buck private."

"Thanks, Gunny."

"You are hearing me, aren't you, Joe? You do know what rides on you and Yahzee, tomorrow?"

Enders nodded.

Hjelmstad returned to his bandolier. "Go get some sleep, Sergeant."

Enders turned and started back, but the Norwegian called out to him: "Hey, almost forgot! . . . Got another letter for you, Enders. Smells real nice, too!"

But Enders didn't reply. Perhaps he didn't hear, due to that bad ear of his; or perhaps he couldn't face another of those damn letters. Maybe he was in no mood of being reminded of a nicer, better world, while he was stuck in this one.

Enders and Yahzee spoke no further that night, and the two men slept on opposite sides of their group within the encampment. No one spoke much, for that matter: the deaths of their fellow warriors, their friends, hung over them, as dark as the black shroud of sky.

Yahzee had established a pattern before settling in to sleep: he checked his M-1 to make sure it was in perfect operating condition; adjusted his helmet to serve as a pillow; and placed his carbine across his body, so that his hand would fall naturally on the trigger, with his combat knife stuck in the ground where his right hand lay, his grenades carefully arranged near his left hand.

One small adjustment to this USMC (as opposed to Navajo) ritual: now his combat knife had been replaced by Whitehorse's twine-wrapped-bone-handled blade.

Dulled by battle, numbed by grief, it did not occur to Yahzee that he had learned this ritual from the man who'd killed Whitehorse.

16

JUNGLE GROWTH RIPPLING ON THE OPEN TERRAIN NEAR THE base of Mount Tapotchau, the Marines of Second Recon edged watchfully through, staying low, keeping quiet. The tall grass undulated, like a nest of snakes, the wind whispering through tauntingly, as if offering warnings that couldn't quite be made out. Chick Rogers, BAR in his hands, as usual walked point, and right now was emerging warily into a muddy clearing, puddles glistening in the early morning light.

Hjelmstad's voice split the silence like a rifle shot: "Chick!"

The Texan froze, boondogger dangling in midair. He looked down and could see it, the glinting metal trigger of a landmine, barely peeking up out of the rain-soaked soil.

As Chick drew his foot back carefully, and set it down the same way, Joe Enders slowly scanned what they now realized was a minefield. These hidden treasures were all around—now that they knew what they were looking for—little mounds, barely visible in the soggy earth. The rainfall had revealed them, just enough, to make this expanse of mud and death traversable . . . maybe.

"I'm betting for every one we can see," Enders said, "there's another we can't."

And the Marines stood petrified in the tall grass at the edge of the muddy expanse beyond which the mountain waited.

"Goddamnit," Pappas said. "Killing me . . . is one thing. . . . Blowin' . . . blowin' my damn balls off is . . ."

But the Greek was sucking in air, starting to hyperventilate.

"Take it easy, Pappy," Hjelmstad said. "Chick got us this far, and he's gonna get us the rest of the way—ain't you, Chick?"

The Texan drew in air, and got out his K-bar and crawled down on his knees, prepared to make a path across the goddamn mud, with the knife as a tool to help locate any mines that weren't immediately obvious. . . .

Chick moved forward gaining ground, getting himself filthy but at least still breathing, Hjelmstad following after. Pappas, however, wasn't budging—his breath was even now, but he seemed unable to will his legs to move, as if the mud were glue.

Just behind him, Yahzee—hauling eighty pounds of radio on his back—gave the Greek a forearm shove. "Move it!"

Pappas damn near lost his balance—not the best idea in a minefield—but finally started ahead, glaring back at the Navajo. "What the hell's eating you, Chief?"

"I ain't no damn chief," Yahzee growled.

Enders, on the Indian's ass, noted this shift in attitude in his codetalker—yesterday's new hardness apparently wasn't temporary, something that could get slept off. He noted, too, how fearlessly Yahzee pushed through the minefield. True, Chick was blazing the way on all fours, but Yahzee wasn't even looking at the muddy ground. . . .

Gunfire—three shots from automatic weapons in the brushy slope beyond—interrupted Enders's musing over whether his codetalker had turned suddenly suicidal. Marines behind him were dropping in the grass, disappearing forever, and those following Chick's lead across the minefield were subject to shots from above that aimed not at them so much as at the mines—one exploded to the left, sending shrapnel and mud flying, then another blew to the right. . . .

Hjelmstad yelled, "Go, go, go, goddamnit!"

And Chick got to his feet, and—mines be damned—hauled ass across the muddy expanse, with Second Recon following under a fusillade of bullets and the exploding earth on either side.

When they had hopscotched over the mines they could make out, and lucked their way past any they could not, Second Recon found themselves on the hardscrabble terrain beyond the muddy minefield. Scatterings of rock provided potential cover, and Enders was ready to fling himself behind an outcropping when Yahzee— fuck!—just kept going, running toward the nearest source of muzzle fire.

Enders had to work to keep pace with the Indian, despite that TBX strapped to his back like a papoose. Yahzee was blasting away with his M-1 up there, killing a Jap who'd been firing from a spider hole.

Two more Japs were firing from a shared spider hole up the slope, and the thing to do, Enders knew, was to haul that dead soldier out and take over the cover the hole offered, and return fire from there . . . but Yahzee, goddamn him, kept running, like bullets weren't being sent his way, both of their ways, and what could Enders do? He had orders. . . .

Yahzee shot one of the Japs in the head and with his Tommy gun, Enders obliterated the other one; and finally the Indian stopped, dropping for cover behind a pile of rocks around the spider hole in which the two Jap corpses slumped blank-eyed. Enders fell in beside his charge.

Jamming fresh ammo in his rifle, noting continuing fire from above, which still sprayed his fellow Marines, Yahzee—his features as immobile and unknowable as a face carved on a totem pole—peered up to pinpoint the source of the bullets.

Breathing hard, Enders studied the man who was hauling around eighty pounds like it wasn't there, and saw the rage in Yahzee's eyes, an anger fueled in part by self-hate, a reckless need to kill that Enders knew only too well.

Then, without warning, Yahzee rushed out and charged up toward a third spider hole—the rocks piled for cover were the tip-off—as if the enemy fire emanating from it were so many firecrackers.

"Yahzee!" Enders yelled. "Shit!"

And, having no damn choice, the bodyguard took off after his codetalker, who showed no sign of even hearing him. Didn't that dumb bastard know that if he got killed, the code died with him, and their recon mission would fail?

As Enders blasted cover fire, following this unlikely point man, the rest of Second Recon trailed after, Hjelmstad leading his men on the run up the unforgiving slope of rock and earth and overgrowth.

A pair of Japanese riflemen were firing desperately at the two Americans rushing toward them, but with Yahzee and Enders on top of them, the Japs couldn't angle their carbines around to properly aim, and the M-1 and, more devastatingly, Tommy gunfire riddled them with lead and filled their spider hole with blood.

As Yahzee dropped to his knees behind a nearby outcropping, first Enders, then the rest of the squad, fell in beside him. Hjelmstad seemed confused—should he reprimand Yahzee, or commend him? Enders realized he had put Gunny in this same awkward position, on their first day of battle on this island.

The lull was shattered by machine-gun fire from above, raining down on them from a nest hidden in the rocks above.

As they returned fire, Enders saw Hjelmstad flinch—he might have been stung by a bee—and thought maybe the gunnery sergeant had taken a minor hit, as both men went back to blasting away, Enders with his Thompson, Hjelmstad with his twelve-gauge.

But within a few moments, Hjelmstad faltered, and fell against Chick.

The Texan paused in firing the big BAR, and his eyes widened, seeing red blossom on Gunny's greens.

"Ah, shit," Chick said. "Viking's hit!"

After sending another burst toward the enemy position, Enders dove over to Hjelmstad, who was already shaking, going into shock, blood spilling from his midsection. Chick was right on it, jamming a hypo of morphine into his sergeant, while Enders ripped open the man's tunic. Moments later a field dressing had been applied to Hjelmstad's wound, Enders pressing it in place, as more machine-gun fire poured down on them.

Risking a peek, Enders got a bead on the enemy position—muzzle flashes, a hundred or so yards away, coming from behind a charred Ha-Go tank twisted into an outcropping—and then ducked back down, reapplying pressure to Gunny's wound. He looked at Hjelmstad, barely conscious, and realized, as on that beach on Guadalcanal, he had again assumed a command.

He was about to bark his first order when he noticed water streaming from Chick's canteen, water tinged red, like cherry Kool Aid . . . only it was from a wound oozing from the Texan's hip. Chick—who was blazing away with his BAR— didn't seem aware of the wound, or maybe was just ignoring it.

Either way, Enders snapped, "Chick, plug that hole, now!"

Still applying pressure to Gunny's midsection, Enders waited as Yahzee threw M-1 fire toward the machine-gun nest and Chick tore open another dressing and jammed the gauze into his bleeding hip.

When Chick had finished, Enders worked his

voice up over the enemy machine-gun fire, bullets kissing rocks all around them and sending up chips and powder. "You okay?" he asked the Texan.

"Never better."

"Can that BAR lay down enough fire to get me a running start?"

"It'll be a fuckin' cakewalk for you, Sarge."

Turning to Pappas, Enders, his voice sharp, still had to yell to be made out over the machine-gun chatter. "Pappy, you and Chick are gonna cover for me. The nest is up behind that wrecked Ha-Go. . . . Yahzee, get over here and keep pressure on Gunny's chest—"

But Yahzee was ignoring the new squad leader, rising up suddenly with M-1 in hand, heavy radio on his back, and a new mission in mind. Enders knew exactly what the codetalker was thinking—he had been in that same suicidal mindset himself, not so long ago—and he grabbed Yahzee by the sleeve, yanking him back.

"Stay down!" Enders ordered.

Yahzee slammed his rifle butt into Enders, knocking him back, a sudden, savage burst of insubordination that stunned Enders—as much for the act itself as its physical violence.

He watched, astounded, as Yahzee leapt over their rock cover and, despite the burden of the radio on his back, sprinted up that slope, the uncertain terrain not slowing him in the least, the Indian unloading his carbine at the enemy, clearing a path with a spray of bullets.

"Cover him!" Enders yelled, yanking off his belt, wrapping it around Hjelmstad's chest, doing his best to staunch the bleeding. "Goddamn you, Yahzee. . . ."

Chick's BAR boomed, the barrel red hot, while Enders leaned over Gunny, who was hanging by the fingertips at the edge of consciousness. Enders commanded him, "Stay awake, you hear?"

Then Enders grabbed his Thompson; his codetalker was out there doing something that might earn the Indian a court martial, or a medal of honor—who knew? The only certainty was, Enders had to back him . . . that was the shit detail he'd been assigned, after all.

"Pappy, Chick," Enders said, "cover my ass, best you can. . . ."

He was about to make his own leap from cover when a trembling hand clutched his dungaree shirtfront.

"Stay . . . stay put, Enders," Hjelmstad said. His eyes were floating. "We can . . . can ride this out till reinforcements. . . . Eighth'll catch up. . . ."

Enders looked behind them; indeed, several columns of Marines were advancing across the tall weeds, toward that minefield, where they would be able to make it across, all right . . . just not soon enough, not near soon enough. . . .

"Afraid not, Gunny," Enders said, shaking his

head. "And don't make it an order—I got other orders, remember? The code that gives us the jump
on the Japs is out there running into their laps."

Hjelmstad's eyes momentarily came into focus—as if he suddenly understood not just what
Enders was saying at this moment, but everything
about the codetalker/bodyguard dynamic; and he
released his grip on Enders's tunic. He even
seemed to nod, a bit—or was that the morphine?

Enders got to his feet, Thompson in his hands
like an extension of himself. He looked at Chick
and Pappas. "This is my command now . . . and
your orders are to stay with Gunny. We got way too
many heroes out here today! *Capeesh?*"

And, not waiting for a response, Enders ran out
after his codetalker, blazing the way with his
Tommy gun.

Pappas, his breathing even now, did not like being left behind; he knew Enders needed the support. Chick was in no condition to join the fray, but
with that big BAR could provide the cover and
company Gunny needed to have a chance.

But Pappas knew he was doing shit, stuck back
here.

The Greek poked his head up and saw Enders
charging ahead, running up the rocky slope after
Yahzee . . . but he also saw a Jap rising up out of
some rocks to take dead-bead aim on Enders, to
the left of the sprinting sergeant. Pappas had no
way to know that this was on the side of Enders's

bad ear; but he could sure as hell tell Enders was in trouble.

Pappas stood, fired a shot, dropped the bastard, and leapt from behind the rocky cover, yelling to Chick, "I gotta give him back-up!"

"Go!" Chick yelled. "I got Gunny."

Then Pappas was in the thick of it, bullets flying, some of them, thank God, his own.

Well up the slope, Yahzee had taken cover behind the metallic corpse of a blown-up half-track. Reloading, wishing he could dump the damn radio—its weight finally registering on him—Yahzee took a deep breath, then leapt out from his cover, staying low, running in a zigzag, firing all the way, as heavier fire flew over his head.

He was heading for cover at the on-its-side wreckage of a bombed-out truck, where a fallen Japanese officer lay in the twisted machinery. Yahzee, charging toward the wreckage, hadn't yet come to a stop when the Jap came to life and swung a katana sword at him.

The Indian pulled back enough to keep from suffering a fatal wound, the blade cutting a flesh-wound groove in his chest, but severing the straps that held the TBX pack on. The radio tumbled to the ground, but Yahzee didn't notice, seeing nothing but the Jap officer, who he shot point blank with the M-1 and, hell with cover, ran on, his chest bare, uniform sliced open, unwittingly leaving behind the radio pack.

About fifty yards behind the Indian, his body-guard had been closing the gap, cutting back and forth in the rocks, shooting from the hip with the Tommy gun. Now Yahzee was moving even faster, though Enders too was unaware, in the clutter of combat, that the radio was a casualty.

Yahzee could see them now, a pair of riflemen and a bipod machine gunner, crouching in the makeshift bunker by the dead Ha-Go on the slope, firing desperately at the zig and zagging fleet-of-foot Marine who took them on with a single carbine.

The codetalker threw himself behind a boulder, breathing hard. He was about fifty feet from the nest. Catching his breath, he unclipped a grenade and yanked the pin. Then he waited for a lull in the gunfire and stood and hurled the pineapple.

The explosion rocked the nest, but fell short, and the enemy guns barely missed a beat, raining fire on the Navajo, who had ducked back behind the big stone as bullets pummeled and powder-kissed it.

Back behind Enders, Pappas—sucking for air, lead flying around him—paused to fire and caught up a slug in the elbow, shattering bone, spinning him off his feet, leaving him on his back, cursing in pain.

Chick had seen this, from the rock-pile position, and yelled "Goddamnit!" and threw more cover fire. Hjelmstad had propped himself up, though barely hanging on, his shotgun in weak hands; he wasn't firing, but he hoped he could protect Chick, if need be . . .

. . . and right now a Jap over to the left, one of those spider hole victims of Yahzee and Enders, was propping himself up, at least as badly wounded as the Norwegian. But the bastard was raising his rifle, to take one more American down before his own death, and Chick—oblivious, blasting away with the BAR—was in the soldier's sights.

It took every ounce of strength left in him, but Hjelmstad pumped his shotgun, and somehow managed to turn the barrel toward that Jap, who saw what Hjelmstad was doing, and re-directed his aim.

Now the two dying soldiers were aiming at each other, dead on, and the two screamed in their native tongues, curses and prayers, the Japanese warrior greeting his ancestors and the Viking going to Valhalla, firing simultaneously, each taking the other's full blast.

Chick whirled, and saw Hjelmstad knocked back, a bullet nestled just above unseeing eyes, and he screamed, *"Gunny."* He fired off a few BAR rounds in rage, then realized his reason for staying behind was gone, and—wound or no wound—he hauled himself and the big weapon out from behind cover, and, leaving his late gunnery sergeant behind, ran toward where the war was—where Yahzee and Enders had taken it.

Up the rocky slope, seeking temporary refuge behind a halved tree, Enders watched that fool Yahzee bearing in on the wrecked Ha-Go; then, shaking his head, Enders sprinted out, Thompson blasting, finally about to catch up with the Indian when the machine gun nest swung its attention— swiveled its barrels—toward him. . . .

As the barrage of bullets sought him, Enders dove behind some rocks, while Yahzee—aware of his bodyguard now—took advantage of the nest's new focus by pulling the pin on his final grenade. His toss this time was a good one, flying over the gutted Ha-Go tank and landing in the midst of the enemy position. The explosion shook the Ha-Go wreckage like a naughty child.

Getting to his feet, Enders took this in warily, peering into the smoke and settling dust, search- ing for Yahzee. The gunfire had ceased, but that makeshift bunker was such that one or more of the gunners within might have dived for sufficient cover to survive the blast. . . .

And just as Enders was thinking of the need for caution, Yahzee seemed to materialize in the swirling dust, running fast, straight for the bunker.

"Ben!" Enders yelled.

But Yahzee either didn't hear him, or maybe just ignored him; either way, the Indian was leaping carbine-first into the smoke-draped enemy nest.

"Shit!" Enders said, and took off running.

Yahzee, within the Ha-Go bunker, saw one of the riflemen, a limp, half-shredded corpse. The machine gunner, however, bloody, near death, was clawing for his holstered pistol and Yahzee shot him as casually as swatting a bug.

That was when the third Jap came out of nowhere, tackling Yahzee, a wild man on the codetalker's back, and the Indian tried to shake him off, but the Jap had something—radio wire!— that got looped around the codetalker's neck, giving the man a stranglehold on him, and Yahzee struggled, air cut off, though he pushed somehow to his feet, and rammed the man against the Ha-Go wall, and then rammed him again.

But the Jap did not give up, a clinching demon, crushing the Navajo's throat, pulling back on the wire. Yahzee was losing focus, getting woozy, fighting to stay conscious; he reached a hand down for the sheathed hunting knife, fingers fumbling on leather. . . .

The enemy yanked back on the wire, squeezed tighter, tighter, and Yahzee weakened, but he managed to unsheathe that blade and put some force into it when he punched the knife into the Jap's thigh.

His assailant screamed, lost his grip, and the Indian whirled, clawing the wire from his throat, and lunged with the bone-handled blade, drawing it back and burying it deep in the man's chest, piercing his heart, killing him damn near instantly.

But when the little corpse tumbled to the earth in the twisted remains of the makeshift bunker, Yahzee climbed on top of him, like a savage, and stabbed him again and again, flailing with the bloody blade.

He sensed a figure coming up behind him, and flew off the corpse, spun toward this new enemy and slashed . . .

. . . and Joe Enders jerked back, though the blade ripped across his chest, cutting cloth, and flesh.

The Navajo was drawing back to strike again, and Enders clutched the codetalker's wrist and, using pressure, forced the knife from his fingers.

"It's me, goddamnit!" Enders said.

Still, blade gone, Yahzee struggled on. Enders, unsure whether or not he'd been recognized—it was almost as if Yahzee were in some kind of trance, or having a fucking fit (but the bodyguard not caring at this point)—threw a forearm into Yahzee's face, sending him reeling.

And as Yahzee fell to his knees, Enders got a new view from the vantage point of the machine nest: thirty yards down the far slope, a Japanese anti-tank gun was pointed right at them.

"Stay down!" Enders yelled, over the *whoosh* of the rocket that was streaking their way.

The shell hit with a deafening impact that seemed to upend the world, but really merely tore the guts out of the Ha-Go, flipping it into the air, stirring up dust and smoke that blotted out everything.

As he staggered to his feet, Enders coughed, kicked away rubble, and peered through the billowing black smoke, searching for his codetalker.

"Ben? Yahzee?"

And as the smoke finally began to clear, Enders saw the Ha-Go—turned over on its side now, with something writhing, someone pinned, underneath its massive twisted metal.

Ben Yahzee.

17

THE TANK'S SHEARED TURRET WAS ON TOP OF YAHZEE'S left leg, and the ground beneath the trapped limb was as much rock as dirt. Pinned there helplessly, the Indian wore an expression betraying neither pain nor concern—Enders would have thought his codetalker was in shock, if it wasn't too soon, and if he didn't know damn well what kind of stubborn craziness the Navajo was wallowing in right now. Enders was, after all, a veteran of such self-pitying stoicism.

They were still draped in the dusky haze of dirt stirred up by the anti-tank shell, and small arms fire cracked all around. The bodyguard got down on his knees in front of his trapped charge.

Words flew out of him: "What the fuck is wrong

with you? You want the Japs to catch you and torture you for the code? You want to get yourself
killed and leave the rest of us without any goddamn communications?"

Yahzee, ignoring the pain, just stared back in
defiance.

"You stupid son of a bitch," Enders said, leaning
in closer, his voice low but heavy with emotion,
"ain't nothing you can do is gonna bring your
buddy back—nothing!"

Yahzee turned away; the pain he could bear,
but these words were too much.

Enders grabbed the Indian by the tunic, with
both fists, and went almost nose to nose with him.
"Ben, goddamnit, I've tried . . . and nothing brings
them back. Nothing. And . . . and nothing can
make them go away, either."

Yahzee's glare softened. It was as if he had seen
something in the bodyguard's eyes he had never
seen before, and Enders felt almost embarrassed
at having revealed so much of himself, though he
was relieved to see some of the hardness in the
Navajo's features, that recent darkness in his eyes,
fade. It was as if Yahzee had been possessed, and
some demon finally left him.

"You white boys talk too much," Yahzee said.
"Help me get the hell out from under this
thing. . . ."

"Thought you'd never ask," Enders said, and he
already had his K-bar out.

Soon they were both digging at the hardscrabble ground around Yahzee's leg, Yahzee using the bone-handled, bloody blade that had been White-horse's, to try to save himself. . . .

Pappas was down the slope, grabbing air at that wrecked half-track where Yahzee had killed the sword-wielding Jap officer. Sitting on a slab of wreckage, Pappas was managing not to hyperventilate, but his arm—that bullet-shattered elbow—was throbbing and hurting like a bitch, under a makeshift dressing he'd applied himself. Tears were welling, and a few streamed down his cheek; he glanced at the dead officer, sprawled there looking right at him, in a frozen grin, a mocking death mask.

"What the hell are you lookin' at, asshole?" Pappas asked.

Then the Greek looked away from the corpse, and noticed something else: Yahzee's radio, the bulky TBX! The long narrow halves of it stacked, strapped together lay upside down, perched on rocks about ten feet away, up the slope, out where bullets were dancing and zinging and powdering the earth and rocks. The radio didn't seem to have taken any significant hits, though, and looked perfectly fine, maybe a dent or two in its dull silver skin.

Pappas crawled out and looked up the hill, searching for Yahzee, and seeing him caught be-

neath the wreckage of that Ha-Go, Enders helping him; he couldn't tell exactly what they were
doing, but it was clear Enders was trying to get
the Indian out from under, digging him out
maybe.

The whiz of bullets invited Pappas to pull back
in and take cover at the half-track wreckage,
where he again looked over at the dead officer.

"Fuck you," Pappas said to the grinning corpse,
and he just sat there, knowing he should go out
and get that radio, and haul it up the hill to the
men who could put it to good use.

Right now Enders was ducking back, rifle fire
from the mountain angling down into the makeshift Ha-Go bunker, finding metal to ricochet off,
bullets bouncing and clanking and clunking all
around. He looked back toward that artillery in-
stallation and saw, hustling up over the ridge below, a Jap rifle squad pushing past the anti-tank
gun, smoke still curling from its big barrel.

"Keep digging," Enders said, positioning himself
with the Thompson, "company's coming."

Yahzee was carving at the rocky ground furi-
ously with the hunting knife, not getting very far.
"How many?"

"Maybe two dozen. . . . Shit!"

Yahzee's eyes flared. "What?"

Enders had seen, beyond the advancing enemy,
the rope netting of camouflage pulling back, re-

vealing more heavy artillery, the kind that made that anti-tank gun seem like a pop-gun: three massive field pieces of a level the U.S. forces had not begun to anticipate.

And at this moment the Eighth Marines were marching up the slopes, with precious little cover in sight. . . .

But right now Enders had to deal with the two dozen enemy charging toward him and his codetalker, firing at them, and he leaned against the side of the dead tank, blasting away at them with the Tommy gun, dropping several, slowing them—they were scrambling for cover, now.

He used the paltry lull to put his Thompson aside and try to get a grip on the heavy twisted metal of the former turret that had Yahzee's leg pinned; and when he had a good grasp on the bastard, he got under it and put all his weight behind the effort . . . and didn't budge it an inch.

Enders could see those big Japanese guns beyond the advancing foe, massive barrels moving, aiming, cranking into position, three huge guns gearing up, taking aim. Enders looked behind him, down the slope, way down . . . where the Eighth Marines advanced, ducks in a barrel for the massive Jap artillery.

Rifle fire started zinging and pinging again, and he snatched up his Thompson and let them have another volley, two more dropping, the others seeking cover, slowing them again, but the Japs were encroaching upon the Ha-Go bunker, closer and closer, their bullets aimed better and better. . . .

"We've got enemy artillery cranking up," Enders said. "Three big pieces—gotta let the Eighth know!"

Yahzee paused in his digging, frowned, and Enders caught that—and realized, at the same time as Yahzee, that the radio was gone.

"Where the hell's the TBX?" Enders demanded.

Yahzee craned to look down the slope and Enders followed his gaze, and there the thing was, upended, caught on some rocks . . . and ten feet beyond it, Pappas was peeking out from behind the shelter of that wrecked half-track, eyeing the radio himself, damn well knowing its importance, and where it needed to go.

Enders threw Pappas a look that was an order, and the Greek wiped the tears and dirt from his face, calming his breathing as best he could; then he burst from cover, running like hell for that radio.

Jap gunners opened up on him from either flank, but Pappas snatched that eighty-pound radio up in his one good arm, that bloody-elbow left of his a useless dangling thing, and despite the weight of his cargo, he zigged and zagged, dodging bullets with supernatural grace, aided by Enders, who had interrupted his protection of the Ha-Go bunker to provide cover for the Greek bearing a gift . . .

. . . who was within a few feet of the bunker

when an enemy bullet cut him down, flinging him rudely onto his back on the rocky earth.

Pappas took a harder fall than the radio, and Enders scrambled to his squadmate, who lay on his back, his breath coming ragged, clawing his paper bag from the breast pocket of his tunic and drawing it frantically to his face, breathing into it.

But the bag didn't expand, air escaping from it, a hole in the brown paper, somewhere—a bloody hole; and both Pappas and Enders saw, at the same time, the wound gouged through his breast pocket, like a deadly button.

They exchanged grim, panicky expressions.

Then Enders twitched a grin and said, "You did good, Pappy."

Pappas smiled, just a little, and then life left his face, and the troubled air eased from his body; swallowing, Enders looked down the slope and, from this vantage point, he could see the Eighth Marines, making a hell of a target in open ground, blowing jungle grass riffling around them.

Enders snatched up the radio and, staying low, scurried back to the Ha-Go bunker with the heavy double-toolbox-like radio.

"They got Pappy," Yahzee said redundantly.

"Pappy got us this," Enders said, and gave the trapped Indian his radio.

"Hang the antennae wire up on top of the tank."

Enders draped the wire up as high as possible,

and said, "Now you get yourself up and running, Ben—the Eighth's down there in open fucking terrain."

"Damn," Yahzee said, fumbling with the big metal boxes.

"I'm gonna spot those Jap guns, and you're gonna call the fly boys in."

Enders knew they had to hold this position, as long as possible; and he had to keep Yahzee alive to call in the coordinates, otherwise that rocky slope would run red with Marine blood. . . .

As he blasted away with the Thompson, Enders could hear Yahzee on the battery-operated radio: *"Wol-la-chee gah tkin besh-do-tliz a-kha tash be-la-sana. . . . Wol-la-chee gah tkin besh-do-tliz a-kha tash be-la-sana. . . ."*

Enders sprayed Thompson slugs at the oncoming squad, and bought himself a lull to check out the position of the three massive guns, looking from it to the sky, trying to figure the angle for an effective bombing run.

"Got to walk 'em in, Ben," Enders said. "They won't see shit from their bird's-eye view."

"Give me the numbers!"

Enders fired another burst, then had another look at the enemy artillery, and did his best to gauge, saying, "Grid two-two-one by one-six-seven."

"Be-al-doh-tso-lani," Yahzee said into the TBX, which in Navajo meant "many big guns." *"Be-al-*

doh-tso-lani—jo-kayed-goh nilchi ba-ah-hot-gli."
The latter meant "request air support," which he
repeated.

Enders was amazed by how quickly the Indian
made this coded transmission, and hoped the
Navajo on the other end, out on the carrier, was as
good and as fast.

Yahzee was rattling off code, now. "*Ah-tad ah-losz a-chi be: da-h gloe-ih a-kha, da-h gloe-ih a-kha, tlo-chin tsah ah-nah be-gha tlo-chin tash ah-nah klesh yes-hes al-na-as-dzoh dibeh dzeh a-keh-di-glini dzeh a-chin.*"

Enders saw the muzzle of that anti-tank gun
flash and, over Yahzee's codetalking, yelled, "Hit
the deck!"

Yahzee covered his head as Enders flattened beside him, as the shell hit nearby, exploding, shaking the world, shrapnel and rock flying.

Rising from the rubble with an idea, Enders
snatched up Yahzee's carbine, trading him the
Thompson, and positioned himself at the metal
wall of the wrecked Ha-Go. He carefully aimed the
M-1 at the Japanese anti-tank team who were
preparing to fire another shell at the makeshift
bunker, and squeezed off half a dozen rounds,
quickly, stitching the quartet with lead, one of
them knocking back into his controls, sending the
barrel downward, firing wildly at their very feet—
blowing them and the anti-tank weapon to hell!

"That felt good," Enders admitted, smiling

tightly, trading weapons back with Yahzee, who was still codetalking.

That trio of bigger guns, however, was beyond Enders's range, and his firepower—and the three artillery pieces each fired, with a devastating one-two-three roar, revetments quivering with the recoil. The big shells whistled over the Ha-Go bunker, shrill, loud, terrible . . .

. . . and train-crash explosions met the forward elements of the Eighth Marines, in the jungle grass, men and materiel crushed under the salvos, obliterated, vaporized.

"Where is that fucking air support?" Enders demanded of the sky.

And the sky answered, a Hellcat cutting across clouds, banking in, powering fast toward those enemy guns. The swift stubby planes could carry incredibly heavy loads, as well as rockets, and it was the latter that this plane sent screaming toward the coordinates Enders and Yahzee had supplied.

The multiple blasts that resulted carved notches in the cliff-face but missed the Japanese guns.

"Airdale came up short!" Enders yelled back at Yahzee. "Goddamn rockets all we got? How 'bout some fuckin' bombs?"

"Give me better numbers," Yahzee said. The Indian, half-pinned under the turret, wearing the head-set, working the radio, waited for Enders to reassess.

Then the bodyguard said, "Drop one hundred, left one hundred!"

Enders was staving off the approaching soldiers with short Thompson bursts, as Yahzee code-talked: *"Be gah a-kha bi-so-dih a-kha tash dzeh lin shi-da tsah be gah ah-jah chindi . . ."*

"Shit!" Enders said, his Thompson clicking on an empty chamber. Yanking out the spent clip, his fingers sought a replacement, but his ammo belt was empty, too.

Yahzee tossed his carbine to Enders, the men exchanged nods, and the Indian went back to it: *". . . Nish-cla-jih-goh d-ah gloe-ih ne-ahs-jah lin shi-da tsah be gah ah-jah chindi."*

Enders barely had the rifle in hand before he was picking off advancing Japs, conserving his ammo, and when he heard the overhead roar of another Hellcat, it was none too soon.

And a full two-thousand-pound payload—no rockets aboard this fighter—dropped into the artillery placement, the first bomb not a direct hit but enough to knock one of the guns out, the second bomb dead center, turning two of the massive artillery pieces into a flying junkyard, taking the Japanese manning it along for a last ride.

Enders let out a war whoop, which caused Yahzee—who was returning to digging himself out with the blade—to raise an eyebrow. The bodyguard picked off the nearest of the Japanese riflemen, inciting a volley from his brothers that sent Enders ducking. But then he jumped back, sighted another rifleman, and clicked on an empty chamber.

Back down for cover again, Enders yanked his pistol from its holster, and began using the last of his ammo sparingly. The remaining riflemen were clinging to their cover—too many of them had fallen under his Thompson and that carbine, and they obviously weren't aware how nearly out of ammo he was.

That was when he noticed the remaining huge gun, its big barrel swinging their way, taking bead right on the Ha-Go bunker, the gunner and his crew readying to fire. . . .

"Son of a bitch," Enders said, and he dove for Yahzee, covering the codetalker with his body.

Another Hellcat came whining overhead— Enders, his bad ear up, didn't hear it, but Yahzee did—and the fighter plane zoomed in to drop another payload on that final big gun. At the last moment, the Jap gunner spotted the Hellcat, and triggered the weapon—but the bomb was already whistling down, right on the money, a thousand pounds of TNT making a miracle shot, the hole-in-one of dive bombing: the shell dropped right down the barrel of the huge gun just as the latter's shell was firing and ordnance met ordnance, creating a cataclysmic explosion and a massive fireball that engulfed the surrounding shells and set them off too, in a series of blasts that virtually exploded the cliffside itself in a hellish blaze of orange and red and yellow and black.

That Enders *did* hear: he crawled off his codetalker, and peered out, seeing the flames and black smoke of the destruction he and Yahzee and the Hellcat had wrought, the guns a bad memory. He looked skyward and the Hellcat tipped its wings to them.

The bodyguard was just allowing himself a smile when a bullet ripped into him.

18

WINCING—THE BULLET HAVING TORN THROUGH HIS bicep—Enders raised the .45 and, with a shot to the head, nailed the advancing rifleman who'd clipped him. The Jap pitched back on the hard earth, leaving a cloud of blood mist where he'd been standing.

Yahzee hadn't seen his bodyguard take that flesh wound, still concentrating on the shale-ridged earth, trying to dig free his left leg from under that tank turret. Carving at the rocky ground, the Indian couldn't believe how little progress he'd made, and when, frustrated, he tried even harder, the tip snapped off the hunting knife.

"Shit!" Yahzee said.

Enders knew the feeling. He'd ducked down as more lead flew their way, and was checking his .45: three rounds left in the clip. He peeked up and saw just one of those advancing Japs blast three rifle rounds his way, as if mocking his three meager remaining bullets. He took cover again, thinking, *damn! Must have been at least a dozen muzzles flashing out there.* . . .

"How's that digging coming?" Enders asked, crouched beside the metal tank wall.

"Not great . . . Joe!"

Enders whirled and two riflemen were coming up at him, just beyond the Ha-Go cover, one shrieking *banzai*-style, and he dropped them with two carefully placed .45 rounds.

In the lull that followed, Yahzee called out, "How many still out there?"

"Not many," Enders said, standing at the twisted metal barrier, and it was true that right now he couldn't see a single Jap—but he knew they were behind every cluster of rocks, every boulder.

"How about the .45?" the Indian asked, carving at the stony ground with his broken knife. "How much ammo you got left?"

Enders didn't reply, his back to the codetalker.

"I guess I know where I stand," Yahzee said.

"You're not standing anywhere, till you get your ass dug out."

And the sound of the blade scraping continued.

Then Yahzee said, "I figure you got at least one bullet left . . . considering your orders."

Enders grimaced. "Shut the fuck up, Ben."

More scraping.

"Kinda quiet out there," the Indian said.

This was where, in war movies, the other guy said, "Too quiet." But Enders was hoping against hope that the silence meant the enemy had fallen back, given up, having read his resistance as a sign of far more firepower than the single .45 slug he had left.

Only, behind those rocks was movement, as the Japs jockeyed into position, edging ever closer. And as Enders was gazing off to the right—that left ear screwing him over yet again—a Jap materialized and, on the run, leapt at their bunker . . .

. . . and Enders, falling back, blasted away, once, put that final bullet in the soldier's brain, knocking him back, sending him sprawling and all Enders could think was, *hell! I should've let him get closer and maybe get his rifle off him.* . . .

Because right now Joe Enders had no weapon, the .45 dropping to the ground from his fingers with a thud.

Between the two of them, in fact, only Yahzee had a weapon: that hunting knife with the sheared point, gritty-looking from chipping and chopping at rocky earth.

"Joe," Yahzee said.

Enders looked at his friend, who had paused in his work.

"You can't let 'em get the code," the Indian said. "I screwed up—pulling this hero shit. Shouldn't be here where they can catch me. . . ."

"I told you to shut the fuck up."

"You follow your orders, Joe. Understand?"

And Yahzee pitched the knife to Enders, the thing turning end over end and dropping in the dirt in a dusty puff at the bodyguard's boondockers.

"Just promise me something," Yahzee said. And he rapped on his helmet with the knuckles of the hand that moments ago held that knife. "The kid I carry around in my hat . . . George. . . . You tell him his pop died a warrior—a good Marine."

But Enders didn't move, dazedly looking down at the knife, then to Yahzee. His shoulders were slumped. Japs were out there behind the rocks. It would be over soon . . . and maybe the bastards wouldn't know Yahzee was a precious commodity, and they could both die as warriors. . . .

"Goddamnit, Joe! Do it!"

Swallowing, Enders—knowing Yahzee was right, and that moments mattered—leaned down and, with a trembling hand, picked up Charlie Whitehorse's blade, streaked with blood and dirt, scarred by stones and shale.

Maybe it was his fucked-up hearing, maybe it was the stress of battle, but the world slowed down for Joe Enders, smoke billowing through like a strange curtain draping their battlefield world, a haze through which he could no longer hear, not clearly anyway, the sounds of war, only the rush of wind, the voice of nature or God or maybe the Navajo gods, trying to send messages.

He glanced back over the Ha-Go wall: the Japs were coming, a little farther back than he'd expected . . . he must have picked off all the closer ones, lurking behind rocks . . . but they were coming, like the Mexicans advancing on the Alamo.

And Enders turned, jaw clenching and unclenching as he began approaching the Navajo, who lowered his gaze, gripping the corn pollen pouch hanging from his neck, whispering a Catholic prayer, hedging his bets, bracing for the inevitable.

Enders fell to his knees and raised that broken but still deadly blade and brought it down with everything he had, burying it deep . . .

. . . into the ground, two inches from Yahzee's chest. The Indian, blinking, not getting it, said, "Joe? What . . . ?"

"Goddamnit, Private, when a sergeant says dig, you fucking dig. Now get diggin'!"

Shaken, Yahzee did as he was ordered, withdrawing the blade from the rocky earth, which he began clawing away at once more, astounded to still be alive.

Enders, in the meantime, was down there putting his hands under that twisted turret, steeling himself for one more try at the goddamn thing, giving it every last ounce of strength he had. He ignored the pain shooting up his arm from the bicep wound, and the burnlike discomfort of where Yahzee had slashed his chest, though blood was spreading, staining his khaki shirt black-red.

Knuckles white, biceps tight, sweat pouring, he made like Atlas and pushed . . . and the turret moved barely a quarter of an inch.

With a grunt, he released the wreckage, and closed his eyes and breathed hard and summoned something within him, something that had nothing to do with religion and everything to do with spirituality as he saw faces float before him—Nells, Anderson, Harrigan, Whitehorse, Pappas . . . and the boys from the Solomons, Mertens and Hasby and Kittring. . . .

Enough goddamn Marines had died under his watch!

Re-setting his feet, like a weight-lifter, he let out a roar and hoisted again and the turret lifted, its dumb weight giving in to Joe Enders's strength of will . . . just an inch, then another, while Ben Yahzee frantically dug with the blade. . . .

"Joe, you're a goddamn wonder!" Yahzee said, digging fiercely.

The wound on Enders's arm was throbbing, pierced muscle tearing; but Enders kept pushing with every bit of sinew he had, veins bulging, cords standing out in his neck. The effort induced a trickle of bloody fluid from his left ear, which trailed down his cheek, though he did not notice, straining even harder, until—somehow—that turret lifted just enough, and Yahzee managed to pull his leg out from under, a moment before Enders had to drop the massive weight, again.

Wincing as feeling rushed into his crushed leg, Yahzee allowed himself to be dragged to his feet by Enders, and the two men—one with a bad leg, the other with a bad arm and a hopeless left ear— made about one damn good Marine between them, hobbling away from the twisted Ha-Go that had been their home and salvation.

By the time the Japanese riflemen got to the abandoned bunker, Enders and Yahzee had a decent lead, the bodyguard dragging the codetalker down the ridgeline, keeping it between them and the Japs as much as possible. Moving like entrants in a potato-sack race, what they did could almost be called running, as they ducked volleys of bullets while traversing the rugged terrain.

But that rocky ground conspired with Enders's shattered eardrum to make the world shift and turn over on itself, drifting out of balance. Still, he stumbled on, not aware that blood and other fluids were seeping from his ruined ear, though well aware of the effort it took, to just put one foot in front of the other.

Then the landscape spun out of control and Enders slipped from Yahzee's grip and tumbled, going down on the stony ground.

Blinking, unsteady even on his knees, Enders was trying to catch his breath and regain his balance when he caught another round, his back arching, face tightening, though Yahzee—doing his best to overcome the consuming pain of his crushed limb—did not notice the bodyguard's new plight.

But the Indian did—despite his mangled left leg—manage to haul Enders back to his feet, and again they stumbled forward, picking their way through clusters of rocks. The Japs, inexorably, were closing the distance, the early lead of the wounded Marines falling away.

Neither the fleeing Marines nor the pursuing Japanese saw Chick Rogers rise up from behind the cover of big rocks; wounded but back in the hunt, he let out a Texas war cry, opening up with his big BAR. The enemy dropped like carnival targets under his heavy fire, as he administered quick, unintentionally merciful deaths.

Yahzee saw Chick now, all right, and—hobbling painfully—pulled Enders back behind the outcropping the Texan had turned into his personal fortress.

Enders, so woozy he didn't realize he'd just been rescued, barked at Chick: "I told you to stay with Gunny!"

"Gunny's dead," the Texan said between BAR

blasts, Japs still falling. "Like these sons of bitches. . . ."

As Chick—a one-man rifle-squad—continued covering them, Yahzee checked his left leg, which had buckled in a manner that suggested numerous breaks, and crushed bone. The pain, however, was manageable—Yahzee realized he was probably in shock—and he turned his attention to his bodyguard.

"You all right, Joe?"

"Aw, you know . . ." Enders was wincing, pale as chalk. ". . . Same old shit, fuckin' ear. . . ."

But Yahzee could see his friend's ear wasn't the only thing bleeding: the front of Enders's tunic was soaking wet, a deep rich blackish red spreading his midsection. Enders had a hand behind him, tight over the entrance wound.

"Wouldn't you just know it," Enders said casually. "One time I turn my damn back. . . ."

"Oh, Joe . . ."

Enders grinned. "You should've seen it, Ben—what our Hellcats did to that cannon. Prettiest goddamn thing I ever saw. . . ."

Then the bodyguard coughed and blood burbled up.

Yahzee dropped the broken knife he'd been gripping all this time, and took his friend's head in his hands, comforting him.

"You just stay quiet," Yahzee said. "Medic'll be here in a flash."

Chick's BAR fire had grown sporadic, the Japs beaten back.

"Get me my smokes," Enders said to Yahzee, "would ya?"

Yahzee withdrew the tarnished USMC-emblazoned cigarette case from Enders's breast pocket, flipped it open—only one remained. For the first time the Navajo noticed the picture in the lid.

After a moment, studying the shot of Enders and his pals in happier times, Yahzee took the home-rolled out of the case and placed it in Enders's lips.

"Zip . . . Zippo's in my pocket," Enders said.

And the lighter was. Yahzee thumbed a flame to hold up where his friend could easily get at it.

Enders drew deep on the smoke, or anyway as deep as his damaged body would allow, and savored the tobacco's flavor. "See the picture in there?"

"Yeah. I saw it, Joe."

"Those are the guys I was tellin' you about . . . Let me see it, would ya?"

"Sure, Joe," Yahzee said, and—with a shaking hand—pulled the picture out of the lid and handed the tattered black-and-white photo to his bodyguard.

Enders looked at the faces, each face, finding comfort in the smiles captured in the picture, including his own. "This guy with his arm around me, Bill Mertens—funniest SOB in the service.

Coulda given Bob Hope a run for the money. . . . Good-lookin' kid in the middle? Al Hasby, real heartbreaker, got more tail than Sinatra. . . . Skinny kid, that's Tom Kittring, Tommy was as serious as a judge but not always as sober, hell of a poker player . . . taught me everything I know. . . ."

"Sound like great guys."

Chick's BAR fire was infrequent now, providing an occasional punctuation mark in their bittersweet conversation.

Enders coughed some more blood, then took another drag on the smoke; the blood on the butt was like lipstick. "Good guys, great guys . . . my friends. Men you fight with, Ben—I mean, we're human. . . . We're gonna become friends, right?"

"Right."

"Nothin' wrong with that."

"Everything's right with it, Joe."

"Anyway. . . ." He coughed again, bloody spittle. "You . . . you asked about 'em, once—that's who they were."

"I'm glad you told me about them, Joe."

A gust of wind came up and snatched the photo from Enders's fingers. He looked after it but when Yahzee reached to retrieve the picture, Enders shook his head, content to let his ghosts float away on the breeze.

"Ben . . . would you . . . tell Rita I read all her letters?"

"Sure. Sure."

The wind whispered to them in its own language; somehow they understood.

Enders locked his eyes with Yahzee's. "Ben . . . did we make any mistakes?"

"I don't remember any, Joe." Then the Navajo smiled, just a little, reassuringly. "You did good."

"We did good."

Yahzee nodded. "We did good."

Enders was straining now, every time he tried to find a breath. Yahzee loosened his friend's collar, making the bodyguard as comfortable as possible.

They could see the ocean from this ridge, and the sun, darting between clouds, painted the ocean with streaks of red and gold. Enders had turned his bad ear toward Chick, so the occasional BAR rounds did not interfere with the sheer natural beauty spread out before him.

Yahzee watched a small miracle take place: the grit of the war, the pain of Guadalcanal, the bloodshed of these tropics, seemed to fade from Enders's features. The man—the soft-hearted soul Yahzee might have encountered in peacetime— was glimpsed.

Enders mumbled something about "friends . . . my friends," and the homerolled dropped from his fingers.

And Joseph F. Enders died, the ocean in his eyes, in the shelter of rocks on a mountainside in Saipan in the arms of his codetalker.

The Texan fired another burst, and peered out into the stony desolation and, seeing no reason to waste any further ammo, called back to the men he was protecting.

"Sarge," Chick said, "I think that's the last of 'em! Sarge . . . ?"

And the boy from Texas looked back at the boy from Arizona hugging the lifeless form of a kid from Philly.

A mist had begun to fall, Yahzee noticed. Still holding Enders tight, he looked up at the sky, to get some of the moisture on his face, letting it calm him, perhaps even forgive him . . . all of them.

Then Chick was next to him, leaning close, and gazed at the peaceful expression on the body-guard's face.

"He's sleeping now," the Texan said. "Finally sleeping . . . those nightmares can't hurt him no more."

Yahzee glanced up, surprised at this sensitivity.

Chick said, "He's gone to a better place, Ben—it's okay. It's okay."

And the Navajo knew the Texan was right, and he let go of his friend, and settled his body on the ground between rocks, hoping the spirit of Joe Enders might at this moment be rising above them, hovering over the mountain, drawn heavenward through the rain and clouds, leaving this world and its stupid man-made wars behind.

19

At the end of World War II, high-ranking policy-makers of the military marked all information related to the Navajo Code—and the existence of the codetalkers themselves—top secret. The Japanese had never broken the code, and it remained valid for future use. Ben Yahzee, like his several hundred fellow codetalkers, was ordered to remain silent about the project, though a few newspaper articles leaked the story about the Navajo Marines, the code itself remaining confidential.

For the peace-loving Dineeh men, these orders were no problem; as codetalker Albert Smith later said, "Talking about war contaminates the minds of those who should not hear about bloodshed." Yahzee agreed: stories of wartime heroism were dangerous, as they might entice the young to think war was something other than hell.

Because of the secrecy shrouding their duties, the codetalkers rarely came home with any additional stripes on their sleeves—even Ben Yahzee, who had delivered Audie Murphy-style battlefield heroics, returned a private first class, his only medal a Purple Heart. Even the original twenty-nine who created the code were not honored.

A number of codetalkers remained in the military (some would eventually serve in Korea), though most boarded trains in San Diego and San Francisco, heading east for their homes and families on the reservation. Though no parades or festivities greeted them—such bragging was contrary to Dineeh culture—the codetalkers were honored with the respect traditional for Navajo warriors.

Many returned to the lives they'd left before enlisting; some, who had lied about their ages to meet Marine requirements, finished high school, while a good number—Ben Yahzee among them—used their veteran's benefits to go to college. And, like all returning combat vets, they did their best to put out of their minds the horrors of war.

Even non-traditional Navajos like Ben Yahzee, however, often sought purification in the Enemy Way ceremony, and Yahzee's own nightmares did not cease until his wife convinced him to seek help from a traditional medicine man.

In 1969, with the advent of computer technology, the Navajo code was rendered obsolete, and the U.S. government finally declassified the code and the existence of the codetalkers. Public recognition at last came about in two annual Marines reunions in May of 1969: one of these, for the Fourth Marine Division, took place in Chicago, and another was held in Hawaii, the Second Marines' 25th Reunion.

A thousand Marines, more or less, and their families, gathered under a crisp blue sky with wisps of clouds that seemed designed to soften the brilliant afternoon sun; nonetheless the blue shimmer of Pearl Harbor took on a gold-metallic glisten that almost hurt the eyes. They had assembled on a grassy hilltop overlooking the modernistic, white, open-air shrine of the USS *Arizona* Memorial—the final resting place for 1,102 crewman who lost their lives on December 7, 1941.

On a stage erected for the occasion, Major Charles Rogers—whose weathered features could not disguise the brash young man he had been, and whose friends still called him "Chick"—stood at the lectern, addressing the group.

"We pay homage today not just to our honored dead," the major said, his voice an easy, confident drawl, "but to those men who are still with us, whose valor and bravery helped preserve this union of people and freedom that we call America."

Behind Major Rogers stood a dozen men in their early and mid-fifties, most looking trim in their Marine uniforms, a few obviously having had to squeeze in a bit. They were Dineeh warriors, these American Marines—codetalkers.

Major Rogers was saying, "This year we at last are able to honor a group of Marines who did their country proud on Guadalcanal, Saipan, Okinawa and Iwo Jima. They stand behind me, their code never broken by the Japanese—their code the only one in the history of warfare never to be broken. Until now, their successes, their sacrifices, have remained unrecognized. . . ."

And from the lectern, Chick Rogers raised a medal and, as he displayed it to the gathering, sun glinted off the rather large bronze medallion. Three inches in diameter, a fourth-inch thick, the medal depicted, at right, the American flag raised by Marines on Mount Surabachi in Iwo Jima (one of the men raising that flag had been a Pima Indian, Ira Hayes). At left, on horseback, in full regalia, riding on the wind, etched in sharp relief, was a Dineeh warrior: "HONORING THE AMERICAN INDIAN MARINE."

The major turned toward the assembled codetalkers, gesturing. "And now I have the honor and pleasure of introducing a man I was proud to serve with on Saipan—a codetalker then, and a professor now . . . chair of Native American History at the University of Arizona, Professor Ben Yahzee."

As applause rang through the afternoon, Ben Yahzee—still boyish despite the years, limping some, from his war injury—approached the lectern. Though Chick smiled, the moment was a solemn one, as the medal—supported by eighteen-inch rawhide thongs strung decoratively with red, white and blue Indian beads—was hung around the Indian's neck, where a pollen pouch already resided.

Chick said, "Congratulations, Ben."

Then the Texan threw his buddy a wink, and stepped back away from the lectern, giving Yahzee his moment, which had been a long time coming.

Yahzee gazed out at the throng of Marines and their families, all those eyes and faces on him, solemn, respectful, waiting to hear what the man who had been chosen to represent the codetalkers with his words would have to say. His wife—still as pretty as a teenage girl—and his son, George Washington Yahzee—almost thirty now, taller than Ben, otherwise his reflection—were smiling at him, obviously proud. George nodded, as if giving his dad permission to begin.

Yahzee unfolded a piece of paper—his prepared speech—then tossed it aside on the lectern. He didn't need a cheat sheet to tell him what to say; the words were in his heart.

"I am proud to be a Marine," Yahzee said, "and I am proud to be of the People, the Dineeh, the Navajo. But I am also proud to be an American."

He clasped the medal, its coolness strangely soothing.

"We will wear these proudly," Yahzee said, "in honor of those who gave their lives for us—and who walk with us still."

Yahzee closed his eyes, willing the tears back. He could have sworn he heard them, Whitehorse and Anderson, their flute and harmonica harmonizing on the wind . . .

. . . And when Ben Yahzee opened his eyes, allowed them to move through the crowd of silent, respectful Marines and their families—here to honor the living and the dead—he saw, he was *sure* he saw, one face that had not changed, not at all.

For several frozen moments—was it the sun?—Yahzee saw an image, black-and-white like an old newsreel, and yet standing there, from across the spiritual divide, as real, as flesh-and-blood as any man here . . . Sergeant Joseph F. Enders, in his dress blues, ramrod straight, proud to be among his fellow Marines, saluting his codetalker, his friend.

And the response was automatic: Ben Yahzee returned the salute.

But when the Indian blinked away his tears, Joe was gone, and only the wind remained.

A Tip of the Helmet

I WOULD LIKE TO THANK EDITORS CAITLIN BLASDELL, April Benavides and Josh Behar who—in addition to providing a strong support system—gave me the opportunity to write this novel.

Mine was one of the first voices in America to champion film director John Woo—many years ago, Asian film expert Ric Meyers introduced me to *A Better Tomorrow* (1986), after which I often wrote about Woo in my movie review column in *Mystery Scene* magazine—and I hope in some small way I've brought a sense of his "heroic bloodshed" style to this novel.

The fascinating premise of the codetalkers and their bodyguards of course has a basis in history, and I am pleased that I was encouraged to expand upon the exciting screenplay by John Rice and Joe Bateer with my own research.

Books consulted on the Navajo war effort include *The Navajo Code Talkers* (1973), Doris A. Paul; *Unsung Heroes of World War II: The Story of the Navajo Code Talkers* (1998), Deanne Durrett; *Warriors—Navajo Code Talkers* (1990), Kenji Kawano; and *Winds of Freedom* (1992), Margaret T. Bixler.

A number of articles, located on the internet, were also helpful, including "The Navajo Code Talkers" by L. C. Kukral of the Navy & Marine Corps World War II Commemorative Committee; "The Navajo Code Talkers" by Gerald Knowles; "Camp Tarawa Monument Honors Vets" by Sergeant Melinda M. Weathers; and profiles on codetalkers William Dean Wilson and Harrison Lapahie. A fascinating documentary, "Navajo Code Talkers: The Epic Story" (1995), directed by Allan Silliphant, was particularly useful. General reference on the Navajos came from *Navajos* (1956), Ruth M. Underhill; *The Native Americans: Navajos* (1978), Richard Erdoes; and *Arizona*, the WPA Guide (1940).

The codetalking in this novel was developed by me, based on numerous dictionaries and vocabulary lists in the above sources; I do not guarantee its authenticity and offer it only as, I hope, a colorful element of the narrative. Similarly, my sources should not be blamed for any inaccuracies, which are my own.

Two of my historical detective novels about private eye Nathan Heller—*The Million Dollar Wound* (1986) and *Flying Blind* (1998)—dealt in part with Guadalcanal and Saipan, respectively, and the bibliographic essays at the back of those novels contain many of the sources of information I used in this novel, as well. A few key references, however, deserve singling out: *Nanyo: The Rise and Fall of the Japanese in Micronesia, 1885–1945* (1988), Mark P. Peattie; *The Great Battles of World War II. Volume I: The Pacific Island Battles* (1985), Charles E. Pfannes and Victor A. Salamone; and *Semper Fi, Mac* (1982), Henry Berry.

Similarly, my Nathan Heller novel *Damned in Paradise* (1996) and the "disaster" mystery *The Pearl Harbor Murders* (2001) include bibliographic essays detailing my reference material on Hawaii and Pearl Harbor. Key reference works here are *When You Go to Hawaii* (1930), Townsend Griffiss; *Roaming in Hawaii* (1937), Harry A. Franck; and *Pearl Harbor Ghosts* (1991), Thurston Clarke.

The internet provided much reference on weaponry, armament, tanks, battles and general World War II matters. Undoubtedly the most helpful articles were "The Invasion of Saipan" by Brian Blodgett and "Breaching the Marianas: the Battle for Saipan" by Captain John C. Chapin, U.S. Ma-